She'd Been Hurt.
She'd Been Lonely. She Needed.

And maybe those were secrets she never meant to reveal to a stranger, but she never told him anything. She just kissed him back, wildly, freely, intimately.

Cameron thought he was a man who took gutsy risks…but Violet was the brave one, the honest one. Something in her called him. Something in him answered her with a well of feeling he'd never known he had.

He raised his head suddenly. "I never meant—"

She gulped in a breath. "It's all right. I didn't think you did."

"It was the moonlight."

"I know."

"I *need* you to know you can trust me."

"I'm thirty-four, Cameron. Too old to trust someone I barely know. But also way too old to make more of a kiss than what it was. We'll just call this a moment's madness and forget all about it."

Easier said…

Dear Reader,

Welcome to another passion-filled month at Silhouette Desire—where we guarantee powerful and provocative love stories you are sure to enjoy. We continue our fabulous DYNASTIES: THE DANFORTHS series with Kristi Gold's *Challenged by the Sheikh*—her intensely ardent hero will put your senses on overload. More hot heroes are on the horizon when *USA TODAY* bestselling author Ann Major returns to Silhouette Desire with the dramatic story of *The Bride Tamer*.

Ever wonder what it would be like to be a man's mistress— even just for pretend? Well, the heroine of Katherine Garbera's *Mistress Minded* finds herself just in that predicament when she agrees to help out her sexy-as-sin boss in the next KING OF HEARTS title. Jennifer Greene brings us the second story in THE SCENT OF LAVENDER, her compelling series about the Campbell sisters, with *Wild In the Moonlight*—and this is one hero to go wild for! If it's a heartbreaker you're looking for, look no farther than *Hold Me Tight* by Cait London as she continues her HEARTBREAKERS miniseries with this tale of one sexy male specimen on the loose. And looking for a little *Hot Contact* himself is the hero of Susan Crosby's latest book in her BEHIND CLOSED DOORS series; this sinfully seductive police investigator always gets his woman! Thank goodness.

And thank *you* for coming back to Silhouette Desire every month. Be sure to join us next month for *New York Times* bestselling author Lisa Jackson's *Best-Kept Lies,* the highly anticipated conclusion to her wildly popular series THE McCAFFERTYS.

Keep on reading!

Melissa Jeglinski

Melissa Jeglinski
Senior Editor, Silhouette Desire

JENNIFER GREENE

Wild in the Moonlight

Silhouette®

Desire

Published by Silhouette Books
America's Publisher of Contemporary Romance

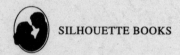 SILHOUETTE BOOKS

ISBN 0-373-76588-6

WILD IN THE MOONLIGHT

JENNIFER GREENE

lives near Lake Michigan with her husband and two children. She has written more than fifty category romances, for which she has won numerous awards, including three RITA® Awards from the Romance Writers of America in the Best Short Contemporary Books category, and a Career Achievement Award from *Romantic Times* magazine.

For Ryan and his bride—

Everyone thinks the romance happens
before you get married, but I promise you two—
the true excitement and wonder and magic come after.

One

Just as Violet Campbell limped inside the back door into the kitchen, she heard the front doorbell ring.

She simply ignored it. It wasn't as if she had a choice. Wincing from pain, tears falling from her eyes, she hopped over to the sink. After spending hours in the brilliant Vermont sun, her kitchen seemed gloomier than a tomb. It wasn't, of course. Her pupils simply hadn't adjusted to the inside light—either that, or the terrible severity of pain from the sting of a particularly ferocious bee was affecting her vision.

Someone rang her doorbell a second time.

Impatiently she yelled out, ''Look! I can't come

to the door because I'm dying, so just chill out for a few minutes!''

Everyone in White Hills knew her, so if they wanted something from her, they were hardly going to wait for formal permission. Heaven knew why she bothered keeping the doorbell operational, anyway. People barged in at all hours without a qualm.

Gingerly she lifted herself onto the red tile counter, kicked off her sandal and carefully, carefully put her right foot in the sink. Her skirt got in the way. Ever since opening the Herb Haven, she'd had fun wearing vintage clothes—her oldest sister claimed she looked as if she shopped from a gypsy catalog. Today, though, she had to bunch up the swingy long skirt to even see her poor foot. An empty coffee cup was knocked over. A spoon fell to the floor. One of the cats—Nuisance? Devil?—assumed she was in the kitchen to provide a lap and some petting.

She petted the cat, but then got serious. Darn it, she needed to get her foot clean. Immediately.

Until that was done, she couldn't tackle the bee sting. She was positive that the stinger *had* to still be in there. Nothing else explained the intense, sharp, unrelenting hurt. Well, there was one other explanation. Friends and family had no idea she was a complete coward, but Violet had discovered three years before that there was one terrific advantage to being divorced and living alone. She could be a cry-baby and a wimp anytime she wanted to be.

And right now, for damn sure, she wanted to be. As far as Violet was concerned, a bee sting justified a sissy fit any day of the week. She dunked her foot under the faucet and switched on the tap. The rush of lukewarm water nearly made her pass out.

Possibly that was taking cowardice too far, but cripes. The whole situation was so unfair—and so ironic. Everything around her seemed to be heartlessly, exuberantly reproducing. Plants. Cats. Socks in her dryer. Even the dust bunnies under the bed seemed to lasciviously multiply the instant the lights turned off at night.

Everybody seemed to be having sex and babies but her—and that sure as sunlight included the bees. Lately she could hardly wander anywhere on the farm without running into a fresh hive. Possibly having twenty acres of lavender coming into bloom might—*might*—have encouraged a few extra bees to hang out. But it's not as if she went close to the lavender. And her normal bees were *nice* bees. They liked her. She liked them.

Not this fella. Didn't male bees die after stinging someone? She hoped he did. She hoped his death was violent and painful and lingering.

The front doorbell rang yet *again*.

"For Pete's sake, could you lay off the doorbell?

I *can't* come to the door, so either come in or go away!''

Bravely gritting her teeth, she squirted antibacterial soap on the injured foot, then screeched when it touched the stinger spot, which was already turning bruisey red and throbbing like a migraine. She forced the foot under the tap water again.

The glass cabinet behind her head contained the box of first-aid supplies, but when she tried to stretch behind her, the movement sent more sharp shooting pains up her leg. The cat had been joined by another cat on the other side of the sink. Both knew perfectly well they weren't allowed on the kitchen counters. Both still sat, as if they were the supervisory audience over an audition she was failing. Her skirt hem kept getting wetter. Her forehead and nape were sticky-damp from the heat—if not from shock. And she noticed the nail polish on her middle toenail had a chip. She hated it when her nail polish chipped.

''Allo?''

The sudden voice made her head jerk up like a rabbit smelling a jaguar in her territory. This just wasn't a kitchen where jaguars prowled. After the divorce, she'd moved home primarily because it was available—her mom and dad had just retired to Florida, leaving the old Vermont homestead clean, ready for family gatherings at any time, but vacant.

She'd made it hers. Not that her mom hadn't had wonderful decorating taste, but she'd fiercely needed to create a private, safe nest after Simpson took off with his extraordinarily fecund bimbo. Now, at a glance, she reassured herself that the world was still normal, still safe, still hers. The old cabinets held a prize collection of red Depression glass. A pot-bellied stove sat on the old brick hearth; she'd angled an antique-rose love seat on one side, a cane rocker on the other—both of which made seats for more cats. Red-and-white chintz curtains framed the wide windows overlooking the monster maple in the back-yard. Potted plants argued for space from every light source. A crocheted heart draped the round oak table.

Everything was normal. Everything was fine... except that she heard the hurried, heavy clump of boots in her hall, coming toward the kitchen, at the same time she heard the jaguar's voice doing that "Allo, allo" thing again.

She didn't particularly *mind* if there was a stranger in her house. No one was a stranger in White Hills for long, and potential serial killers probably wouldn't call out a greeting before barging in. Still, she didn't know anyone who said "allo" instead of "hi" or "hello." It wasn't the odd accent that rustled her nerves but something else. There was something...spicy...about that voice. Something just a little too sexy and exotic for a somnolent June afternoon in a sleepy Vermont town. Something that made her knees feel buttery.

On the other hand, Violet knew perfectly well that

she was a teensy bit prone to being overdramatic, so it wasn't as if she felt inclined to trust her instincts. Reality was she was more likely stuck with a visitor—and right now she just had no patience with any more complications.

Without even looking up, she snapped out, "My God, you nearly scared me half to death. Whoever the hell you are, could you reach in the cupboard behind my head? Second shelf. I need tweezers. First-aid cream. And that skinny tube of ammonium stuff for stings. And the plastic bottle of purple stuff that you wash out wounds with, you know, what's it called? Or maybe hydrogen peroxide. Oh, cripes, just give me the whole darn box—"

The stranger interrupted her list of instructions with that quiet, dangerous voice of his. "First— where exactly are you hurt?"

Like she had time for questions. "I'm not just *hurt.* I'm in agonizing pain. And I always tell myself that I should stockpile pain pills and narcotics, only damn, I never take any. I don't suppose you carry any morphine on you?"

"Um, no."

"I suppose you think it's crazy, my talking this way to a stranger. But if you're going to rob me, just do it. Feel free. I don't even care. But get me the first-aid box first, okay?"

Silence. Not just on his part, but on hers. It was one thing to believe she was totally okay with a stranger in her kitchen, and another to have said stranger suddenly show up between her legs—before they'd even been introduced yet.

She gulped.

Close up, the guy could have sent any woman's estrogen levels soaring. He seemed to cross the room so fast, and suddenly his blond head was bent over her foot in the sink. He was built long and sleek, with a daunting shoulder span and arm muscles that looked carved out of hickory. His feet alone looked bigger than boats. His hair was dark blond, disheveled, longish, as if he'd been outside in the hot breeze for hours. She couldn't see much of his face except for his profile—which amounted to one hell of a nose and skin with a deep tan. The khaki shirt and boots and canvas pants were practical, not fancy, and though he was lean, he looked strong enough to knock down walls for a living.

When he finally glanced at her face, she caught the snap and fire of light-blue eyes, and a narrow mouth that seemed determined not to laugh. "All that yelling," he said finally, patiently, "was about this sting?"

"Hey. It's not *just* a sting. You didn't see the bee. It was huge. Bigger than a horse. Practically bigger than an elephant. And it—"

"Are you allergic to bee stings?"

"No. Good grief, no. I'm not allergic to anything.

I'm totally healthy. But I'm telling you, this was a big bee. And I think the stinger's still in there.''

"Yeah, I can see it is." Again he lifted his head. Again she felt those amused blue eyes pounce on her face, and caught a better look at him. That shag of blond hair framed a long-boned face that looked carved by a French sculptor.

If she wasn't dying from misery, she might have let a shiver sneak up her spine. One look—and no matter how soggy her mind was from the pain—she was absolutely positive this guy wouldn't normally be running around White Hills, Vermont...or any other back-country town.

"For the record," she said, "you're lost."

"You think?" He shifted behind her, opened the cabinet and promptly hefted down her first-aid box. Well, actually, it was a shoe box. Filled to overflowing with herbal, natural, artificial and any other kind of first-aid supplies she'd accumulated over the past three years—and probably a few her mom had had around for the thirty years before that. He located the tweezers first.

The way the stranger held the tweezers made her nervous. Either that or something else did. Either way, she was really starting to get seriously nervous, not just pretend—and darn it, she hadn't been doing all that well before the exotic stranger barged in.

"You're lost," she repeated. "I'm Violet Campbell. I own the Herb Haven—the building and greenhouses on the other side of the yard. This is my house. If you'll tell me who you're trying to find, I'll be glad to—*eeeikes!*''

He lifted the tweezers to show her the stinger. ''It looks like the stinger of a little sweat bee.''

Violet pinched the skin between her brows. Another delightful advantage to being divorced, apart from removing the scoundrel from her life, was not having to put up with men's sick sense of humor. ''Who are you looking for?'' she repeated.

''You.''

He lifted the brown bottle of hydrogen peroxide and started unscrewing the top. She suspected he was going to pour it on the wound. She also suspected that she was going to shriek when he did—and maybe even cry. But the way he said ''you'' in that sexy, exotic accent put so much cotton in her throat that the shriek barely came out a baby's gasp.

''See, that wasn't so bad, was it? The stinger's out. The spot's clean. Now you might want to take an antihistamine or put some ice on the spot for a few minutes—''

''You couldn't possibly want me,'' she interrupted. And then pinched the skin between her brows a second time. On any normal day she liked people. She liked interruptions. She even liked a hefty dose of chaos in her life. But there were men she felt comfortable with and men she didn't.

This one was definitely a ''didn't.'' He made her

feel naked, which was pretty darn silly considering she was dressed in the ultramodest clothes of another era—except she suddenly realized her skirt was hiked up past her thighs. The point, though, was that she most certainly wasn't wearing male-attracting clothes. Her women customers got a kick out of her sense of style, but men almost always backed away fast.

That was how she wanted it. She liked guys, had always liked guys, but she'd been burned enough for a while. Maybe for a whole lifetime. Normally men noticed her clothes and immediately seemed to conclude that she was a little kooky and keep their distance, so God knew what was wrong with this stranger. He'd surely noticed the oddball long skirt and vintage blouse, but he was still looking her over as if she were meringue and he had a sweet tooth.

Momentarily, though, he went back to playing doctor, scrounging in her first-aid box until he found the ammonium wand for bites and stings. She winced even before he'd touched the spot. As if they were in the middle of a civilized conversation, he said, "You were expecting me."

"Trust me. I wasn't expecting you."

"I'm staying here for a few weeks. With you."

The wince was wasted. When he touched the wound with the ammonium wand, she sucked in every last dram of saliva her throat had left and released a screech. A totally unsatisfying screech. The ammonium hissed and stung like—damn it. Like another bee sting. Only worse. Still, she'd somehow easily managed to keep track of the conversation this time. "Obviously, you're not staying here. I don't even know you. Although I'm beginning to think you're a complete maniac—"

Actually, she wasn't particularly afraid of maniacs. She took credit for being one herself often enough. But she'd lost the last of her usually voluble sense of humor with that bite of ammonia. Good-looking or not—sexy or not—she was really in no mood for an emotional tussle with a stranger.

The man swooped everything back in the first-aid box, then turned around and aimed for the freezer, obviously to find some ice. "My name is Cameron Lachlan."

"Great name. I'm happy for you."

He grinned, but he also kept moving. When she motioned to a lower cupboard, he bounced down on his heels and came up with small baggie for the ice. "We definitely have some kind of strange screwup going on here. You *do* have a sister named Daisy Cameron, don't you?"

It wasn't often she got that thud-thud-thud thing in her stomach, but her palm pressed hard on her tummy now. "Yes, for sure. In fact, I have two sisters—"

"But it's Daisy who lives in France."

"Yes, for several years now—"

"The point being," he said patiently, "that your sister has been playing go-between for us for months. Or that's what I've understood. Because she was living right there, and because she knows my work and me personally, so you wouldn't have to be dealing with a stranger. You were supposed to be expecting me. You were supposed to have a place for me to stay for several weeks. You were supposed to know that I was arriving either today or tomorrow—"

"Oh my God. *You're* Cameron Lachlan?"

He scratched his chin. "I could have sworn I already mentioned that."

It came on so fast. The light-headedness. The stomach thudding. The way her kitchen suddenly blurred into a pale-green haze.

Granted, she was a coward and a wuss—but normally she had a cast-iron stomach. Now, though, when she pushed off the counter and tried to stand on both feet, her bee sting stabbed like hot fire and her stomach suddenly pitched. "Try not to take this personally, okay?" she said. "It's not that I'm not glad to see you. It's just that you'll have to excuse me a minute while I throw up."

Two

Once Violet disappeared from sight—presumably to find the nearest bathroom—Cameron leaned against the kitchen counter and clawed a hand through his hair. Talk about a royal mess. What the hell was he supposed to do now?

Nothing usually rattled him. Normally people got a higher education to earn a better living. Cameron had pursued a Ph.D so he could enjoy a footloose, vagabond lifestyle. He was used to jet lag. Used to time changes and strange beds. He had no trouble getting along with people of all different backgrounds and cultures.

But this blonde was doing something to his pulse.

"Be careful with my sister," Daisy had warned him—which, at the time, had struck him as a curious thing to say. His only interest in Violet Cameron was business. Still, whether he'd wanted to hear it or not, Daisy had filled in enough blanks for him to understand why she was so protective of her younger sister. Violet had apparently been married to a real, selfish creep. "Something happened in that marriage that I still don't know about. Something really bad in the last year. I still can't get her to talk about it," Daisy had told him. "But the point is, Violet was always extra smart, in school and life and everything else. It's just since the divorce that she's been…different. Fragile and nervous about men."

Since that conversation had at the time been none of his business—and none of his interest—Cameron had pretty much forgotten it. Still, he'd definitely imagined a shy, quiet, understated kind of woman. A true violet in personality as well as name.

Now he wondered if Vermont might secretly be an alternative universe. Granted, he'd only been in the state for a couple of hours—and on the Campbell property even less than that—but Daisy's description didn't match anything he'd noticed in reality so far. Violet was as shy as neon lights, as nervous as a lioness, and as far as IQ…well, maybe she was smart, even ultrasmart, but who could tell beneath all those layers of ditsiness?

He heard a door open and instinctively braced.

Seconds later Violet walked back in the kitchen. When she spotted him leaning against the counter, she seemed to instinctively brace, too.

Considering that Cameron had always gotten on well with women, it was a mighty blow to his ego to make one sick on sight. At the vast age of thirty-seven, though, he never expected to respond to a woman with a tumbly stomach of his own.

The old Vermont farmhouse seemed sturdy and serious. At first glance, he'd thought the base structure had to be at least two centuries old. The brick surface had tidy white trim and a shake roof; the plank floors were polished to a high shine. He'd been drawn to the place on sight; it looked practical and functional and solid, nothing frivolous.

Only, then there was her.

Standing with the light behind her, she could have been a fey creature from a fairy story. The first thing any breathing male was going to notice, of course, was her hair. It was blond, paler than sunlight, and even braided with a skinny silk scarf, it bounced halfway down her back...which meant it had to reach her fanny when it was undone. Her face was a valentine with warm, wide, hazel eyes, sun-kissed cheeks and a nose lightly peppered with freckles.

She wasn't exactly pretty. She just had that *something*. Some kinds of women just seemed born pure female. They were never as easy to get along with— much less understand—but they seemed to radiate that female thing from the inside out. Nothing about her was flashy or sexy, but she was sensual from that pale, shiny hair to her soft mouth to the rounded swell of her breasts.

She seemed to be wearing old clothes—not old, as in practical, but old, as in the stuff you'd find in a great-grandmother's attic trunk. The white blouse completely covered those delectable breasts, but the fabric seemed less substantial than a handkerchief. It was tucked into a long skirt swirling with bright colors. Crystal earrings dangled to her shoulders. A couple of skinny bangle bracelets glinted on her wrist. There was nothing immodest about the clothes; if anything, they seemed unnecessarily concealing for a sultry, ninety-degree afternoon. Cameron just wasn't sure what the vintage gypsy image was supposed to mean.

He also couldn't help but notice that she smelled.

Guys weren't supposed to mention that sort of thing, but smells were Cameron's business—and had helped him put away a sizable bank account—so scent tended to be a priority for him. In her case, she wasn't using the kind of perfume that came out of a bottle, but around her neck and wrists there was the sweet, vague scent of fresh flowers—as if she'd ambled into a garden with roses and lilac petals and maybe some lily of the valley.

He noticed the delicate scents—which helped him forget that he'd also noticed her spanking-orange underpants. Usually he knew a woman just a wee bit better before he'd gotten a look at her underwear, but when Violet had been on the counter, trying to wash her foot in the sink, she'd pushed up her skirts—no reason for her to have been thinking about modesty since she obviously hadn't been expecting company.

Hell. He hadn't planned on barging in without being asked, either, but when a woman yelled out that she was dying, he could hardly stand on her front porch and wait politely for further news bulletins.

Now, though, she frowned at him. "We seem to be in quite an uh-oh situation," she announced.

That wasn't quite how he'd have put it, but he sure agreed. "You'd better get your foot up before that sting swells up on you."

"I will."

"You're not still feeling sick to your stomach, are you?" He wanted to directly confront their obvious problem, but since she'd established—incontestably—that she was a hard-core sissy about the bee sting, it seemed wise to get her settled down. He sure as hell didn't want her keeling over on him.

"I think my stomach's fine now. It doesn't matter, anyway. What matters is that we have to figure this out. Your being here. What we're going to do with you."

"Uh-huh. You want me to get us a drink?"

"Yes. That'd be great." She sank into a chair at the oak table, as if just assuming he could find glasses and drinks. Which he could. He just didn't usually walk in someone's house and take over this way.

Being in the kitchen with her was like being assaulted with a rocket full of estrogen. It wasn't just that she was a girly-girl type of woman, but everything about the place. Cats roosted on every surface—one blinked at him from the top of the refrigerator; another was sprawled on some newspapers on the counter; a black-and-white polka-dotted model seemed determined to wind around his legs. Every spare wall space had been decorated within an inch of its life, with copper pots and little slogans over the door and wreaths and just *stuff*. From the basket of yarn balls to heart-shaped rag rugs, the entire kitchen was an estrogen-whew. The kind of a place where a guy might be allowed to sip some wine, but God forbid he chug a beer.

On the other hand, he found lemonade in the fridge in a crystal pitcher. Fresh squeezed. The refrigerator was stuffed with so many dishes that he really wanted to stand and stare—if not outright drool. Never mind if she was overdosed with sex appeal. He might get fed out of this deal. That reduced the importance of any other considerations...assuming either of them could figure out how to fix such a major screwup.

"I think we need to start over," he suggested. "You seemed to recognize my name? So I assume you also know that I'm the agricultural chemist from Jeunnesse?''

She immediately nodded at the mention of the French perfume company, so at least Cameron was reassured there was some cognition and sense of reality between her ears. But somehow she looked even more shaken up instead of less.

''I just can't believe this. I *did* know you were coming, Mr. Lachlan—''

''Cameron. Or Cam.''

''Cameron, then. What you said was very true. My sister's called and written me several times about this.'' She lifted her bee-stung foot to a chair and accepted the long, tall glass of lemonade he handed her. ''I'm just having a stroke, that's all. The timing completely slipped my mind.''

''You have twenty acres of lavender almost ready to be harvested, don't you?''

''Well, yes.''

Cameron took a long slow gulp of the lemonade. It seemed to him that it'd normally be a tad challenging to forget twenty acres of lavender in your backyard.

''You're supposed to want me here,'' he said tactfully.

''I do, I do. I just forgot.'' She raised a ring-spangled hand. ''Well, I didn't just *forget*. It's been unusually chaotic around here. Our youngest sister,

Camille, got married a couple weeks ago. She'd been here most of the spring, working on the lavender. And she left on her honeymoon. Only, then she came back to get the kids."

Boy, that made a lot of sense.

"Cripes, I don't mean *her* kids. I mean her step-kids. Her new husband had twin sons from a previous marriage. And actually since Camille thinks of them as hers, I suppose it's okay to call them her sons directly, don't you think?"

Cameron took a breath. As thrilling as all this information was, it had absolutely nothing to do with him. "About the lavender…" he gently interrupted.

"I'm just trying to explain how I got so confused. I started the Herb Haven three years ago, when I moved back home, and it's done fine—but it was this spring that it really took off. I've been running full speed, had to hire two staff and I'm still behind. And then Camille needed me to do something with all their dogs and animals while the family was on the honeymoon— I mean, they got a few days to themselves, but after that they even invited the kids and his dad, can you believe it? And then this old farmhouse I try to keep up myself. And then there are the two greenhouses. And Daisy…well, you already know my older sister, so you know Daisy's genetically related to a steamroller."

Finally she'd said something that Cameron could connect to. Daisy was no close personal friend, only a business connection, but he'd spent enough time to believe the oldest Campbell sister could manage a continent without breaking a sweat. Daisy was a take-charge kind of woman.

"Anyway, the point is, sometimes Daisy runs on—"

"*Daisy* runs on?" Cameron felt that point needed qualifying. As far as he was concerned, Daisy couldn't touch her younger sister for her ability to talk—extensively and incessantly.

Violet nodded. "And I just don't always listen to her that closely. Who could? Daisy always has a thousand ideas and she's always bossing Camille and me around. We gave up arguing with her years ago. When you've got a headstrong horse, you just have to let them run. Not that I ride. Or that Daisy's like a horse. I'm just trying to say that it's always been easier to tune out and just let her think that she's managing us—"

"About the lavender," Cameron interrupted again, this time a wee bit more forcefully.

"I'm just trying to explain why I forgot the exact time when you were coming." She hesitated. "I also seemed to have forgotten exactly what you're going to do."

Before he could answer, someone rapped on her front door. She immediately popped to her feet and hobbled quickly down the hall. Moments later she came back with her arms full of mail. "That was

Frank, the mailman. Usually he just puts it in the box at the road, but at this time of year, there can be quite a load—''

More news he couldn't use. And before he could direct her attention back to the lavender, her telephone rang. Actually, about a half dozen telephones rang. She must have a good number of receivers, because he could hear that cacophonic echo of rings through the entire downstairs.

She took the kitchen receiver—which enabled her to pet two cats at the same time. Possibly she was raising a herd, because he hadn't seen these long-haired caramel models before. The caller seemed to be someone named Mabel, who seemed to feel Violet could give her some herbal suggestions for hot flashes.

This took some time. Cameron finished one glass of lemonade and poured another while he got an earful about menopause—more than he'd ever wanted to know, and more than he could imagine a woman as young as Violet could know. What was she, thirty? Thirty-one? What in God's name was squaw root and flax seed oil?

She'd just hung up and turned back to face him when the sucker rang again. This time the caller appeared to be a man named Bartholomew. Although she seemed to be arguing with the guy, it was a stressless type of quarrel, because she sorted through her mail, petted more cats and put breakfast cups in the dishwasher during the conversation. A woman could hardly be ditsy to the bone if she could multitask, right? Then she hung up and started talking to him again.

"You see?" she asked, as if there was something obvious he should be seeing. "That's exactly why it's impossible for you to stay. Bartholomew Radcliffe is supposed to be putting a new roof on the cottage. The place where you were going to stay when you came in July."

"It *is* July," he felt compelled to tell her.

She made a fluttery motion with her hand, as if the date were of no import. Clearly there were several things in life that Violet Campbell considered inconsequential—dates, facts, contracts and possibly anything else in that generically rational realm. Because he was starting to feel exhausted, he rested his chin in his hand while she went on.

"That's exactly the thing about July. The roof was supposed to be done by now. It's just a little cottage. How long can it take to put a roof on one little cottage? And Bartholomew promised me it'd only take a maximum of two weeks, and he started it way back near the first of June. Only, I've never worked with roofers before."

"And this is relevant, why?"

"Because I had no idea how it was with them. Today he didn't come because there's a threat of rain." She motioned outside to the cloudless sky.

"He doesn't come on Fridays because Friday apparently isn't a workday. And then there's fishing. If the fishing's good, he takes off early. You see what I mean?"

What he saw was that Violet Campbell was a sexy, sensual, unfathomable woman with gorgeous eyes and silky blond hair and boobs that he'd really, really like to get to know. The only problem seemed to be the content under her hair. There was a slim possibility she could fill out an application at a nut house, and no one would be certain whether she wanted employment or an inmate's room.

"I don't suppose there's any chance you'd like to talk about the lavender crop." But by then, he should have realized that Violet couldn't be tricked, coaxed or bribed into staying on topic.

"We *are*. Basically. I mean, the issue is that when—if—you came, I assumed you could stay at the cottage. It's nice. It's private. It's comfortable. But it's quite a disaster right now because they had to take off the old roof to put on the new one. So there's dust and nails everywhere. And tar. That tar is really hot and stinky. So the place simply isn't livable. It will be— In fact, I can't believe it'll take him more than another week to finish it—"

"Depending on his fishing schedule, of course."

"Yes. Exactly."

"Well, I'm hearing you, chère. But it'd be a wee bit tricky for me to fly all the way back to France, just to wait out Bartholomew's fishing schedule. And although I understand your strain of lavender runs late, I absolutely have to be here for the first of the harvest.''

"Well, yes, that's all true, but I'm just confused what I can possibly do with you until I've got a place for you to stay."

Maybe jet lag was getting to him. Maybe at the vast age of thirty-seven, he was no longer the easy-care, rootless vagabond he used to be. Maybe missed sleep and strange mattresses had finally caught up with him…but it seemed pretty damn obvious that Violet couldn't really be this flutter-brained. Something must be bothering her about his being here. He just had no idea what. Considering her older sister had okayed him, she couldn't be afraid of him, could she?

Nah. Cameron easily dismissed that theory almost before it surfaced. It wasn't as if all women liked him. They didn't. But he got along with most, and those women who related to him sexually generally were afraid that he'd have taken a fast powder by morning—no one was afraid of him in any other sense, that he could imagine.

So he slowly put down his lemonade glass and hunched forward, deliberately making closer eye contact. Not to elicit any sexual response, but to encourage an eye-to-eye honest connection. "Violet," he said slowly and calmly.

"What?"

"Quit with the nonsense."

"What nonsense?"

"Sleeping arrangements are not a problem. I wouldn't mind sleeping outside on the ground. Actually, I like sleeping under the stars. Hell, I've roughed it on four continents. And if we get into some stormy weather, I'll find a hotel in town and commute. My finding a place to throw a pillow is no big deal. So is there some reason that you don't want me here that you haven't said?"

"Good heavens. Of course not—"

Again, he said slowly and carefully, "You are aware that my work with your lavender is potentially worth thousands of dollars to you? Potentially hundreds of thousands?"

She squeezed her eyes closed briefly—and when she opened them again, he read panic in their deep, dark, beautiful, hazel depths. "Oh God," she said, "I'm afraid I'm going to be sick again."

Three

"No, you're not going to be sick again," Cameron said emphatically.

Violet met his eyes. "You're right. I'm not," she said slowly, and took a long deep breath.

She had to get a grip. A serious grip. She wasn't really nauseous, she was just shook up. Her foot throbbed like the devil—that was for real. She'd been running all day in the heat even before the bee sting—that was for real, too. And normally men didn't provoke her into behaving like a scatterbrained nutcase—but there were exceptions.

Virile, highly concentrated packages of testosterone with wicked eyes and long, lanky strides were a justifiable exception.

Violet tried another deep, calming breath. Most blondes hated blonde jokes, but she'd always liked them. She knew perfectly well how she came across to most men. A guy who thought he was dealing with a ditsy, witless blonde generally ran for the hills at the speed of light, or at the very least, considered her hands-off—and that suited Violet just fine.

It was just sometimes hard to maintain the ditsy, witless persona. For one thing, sometimes she actually felt ditless and witsy. Or witless and ditsy. Or…oh, hell.

That man had eyes bluer than a lake. She did much, much better with old, ugly men. And she did really great with children. Not that those attributes were particularly helping her now.

But that grip she'd needed was finally coming to her. Those long, meditative breaths always helped. "I have an idea," she said to Cameron. "You've traveled a long way. You have to be hungry and tired—and I'm the middle of an Armageddon type of afternoon. Could you just…chill…for an hour or so? Feel free to walk around…or just put your feet up on my couch or on the front porch. I need to walk over to my Herb Haven, tell my employee what's happening, finish up the problems I was in the middle of, get closed up for the day."

"Is there anything I could help you with?"

"No. Honestly. I just need an hour to get my life back in order…and after that I've got more than enough in the fridge for dinner. I can't guarantee it's something you'll want to eat, but we could definitely talk in peace then—''

"That sounds great. But if there's running I could do for you, say. I know you can't want to be on that foot.''

"I won't be for long.''

It worked like a charm. She just couldn't concentrate with all those life details hanging over her head—and with an impossibly unsettling man underfoot. An hour and a half later, though, she was humming under her breath, back in her kitchen, her one foot propped on a stool and a cleaver in her hand big enough to inspire jealousy in a serial killer.

Not that any foolish serial killer would dare lay a hand on one of her prized possessions.

She angled her head—just far enough to peer around the doorway to check on her visitor again. There was no telling exactly when Cameron had decided to sit down, but clearly it was his undoing. He'd completely crashed. He wasn't snoring, but his tousled blond head was buried in the rose pillow on the couch, and one of his stockinged feet was hanging over the side. That man was sure *long*. One cat— either Dickens or Shakespeare—was purring on the couch arm, supervising his nap with a possessive eye.

Amazing how easy it was for her to relax when he was sleeping.

She went back to her chopping and sautéing and

mixing. Cooking was a favorite pastime—and a secret, since she certainly didn't want anyone getting the appalling idea that she was either domestic or practical. Tonight she couldn't exercise much creativity, because she already had leftovers that needed using up, starting with some asparagus soup—and somehow finding an excuse to eat the last of the grape sorbet.

Early evening, the temperature was still too sweltering to eat anything heavy, but it was no trouble to put together bruschetta and some spicy grilled shrimp for the serious part of the meal. The shrimp took some fussing. First seeding and slicing the hot chilies. Then slicing the two tall stalks of lemongrass. Then she had to grate the fresh ginger, crush the garlic, chop the cilantro and mix it with warmed honey and olive oil.

He'd probably hate it, she thought. Men tended to hate anything gourmet or fancy, but as far as Violet was concerned, that was yet another of the thrilling benefits to being divorced. She could cook fancy and wild all she liked—and garlic-up any dish to the nth degree—and who'd ever care?

She'd have belted out a rock-and-roll song, off-key and at the top of her lungs, if it wouldn't risk waking her visitor. She'd deal with him. But right now she was just seeping in some relaxation, and satisfaction. She'd kicked some real butt in the last hour, finished up the week's bookkeeping, made up

four arrangements for birthday orders and fetched a
van full of pots and containers from town. Even without the bee sting, it was a lot to do for a woman who
was supposed to be a flutter-brained blonde, but then,
when no one was watching she had no reason to be
on her guard.

Her sisters thought she was afraid of getting hurt
again because of Simpson. The truth was that her ex-
husband had turned out to be a twerp, but she never
held that against the other half of the species. She
wasn't trying to avoid men. She was trying to help
men avoid her—and for three years she'd been doing
a great job at it, if she said so herself.

She was still humming when the telephone rang—
naturally!—just when she was trying to coat the
shrimp with the gooey mixture. She cocked the receiver between her ear and shoulder. "Darlene! Oh,
I'm sorry, I forgot to call you back…and yes, you
told me he was a Leo. Okay. Try a fritatta with flowers. Flowers, like the marigolds I sold you the other
day, remember? I'm telling you, those marigolds are
the best aphrodisiac…and you wear that peach gauze
blouse tonight…uh-huh…uh-huh…"

Once Darlene Webster had been taken care of, she
washed her hands and started stabbing the coated
shrimp on skewers. Immediately the phone rang
again. It was Georgia from the neighborhood euchre
group. "Of course I can have it here, what's the dif-

ference? We'll just have it at your house next time. Hope the new carpet looks terrific.''

After that Jim White called, who wanted to know if he could borrow her black plastic layer. And then Boobla called, who wanted to know if there was any chance Violet could hire her friend Kari for the summer, because Kari couldn't find a job and they worked really well together. Boobla could talk the leaves off a tree. Violet finally had to interrupt. ''Okay, okay, hon. I've got enough work to take on one more part-timer, but I can't promise anything until I've met her. Bring her over Monday morning, all right?''

She'd just hung up, thinking it was a wonder she wasn't hoarse from the amount of time she got trapped talking on the phone, when she suddenly turned and spotted Cameron in the door.

Her self-confidence skidded downhill like a sled with no brake.

It was so unfair. Cameron had been in a coma-quality nap; she knew he had, so you'd think he'd have woken up still sleepy. And he yawned from the doorway, but she still felt his eyes on her face like sharp, bright lasers. Interested. Scoping out the territory from her disheveled braid to her bare feet.

''You're a hell of a busy woman,'' he said. His tone was almost accusing, as if she'd misled him into thinking she was too scatterbrained to maintain any kind of serious, busy life.

"I'm sorry if the phone woke you. It's been hell coming back to the town where I grew up, because everyone knows me." She added quickly, "Are you hungry? All I have to do is pop the shrimp on the grill and I'm ready—"

"I'll do it, so you can stay off that hurt foot."

Whenever *she* woke up from a nap, she had cheek creases and bed hair and a crab's mood until she got going again. He seemed to wake up just as full of hell and awareness as when he'd dropped off. There was no way she could like a man with that kind of personality flaw. Worse yet, he proved himself to be one of those easygoing guys, the kind who rolled with the punches and tended to fit in whatever kind of gathering they walked into. He started her grill before she could—and the barbecue was one that could make her mother swear; it *never* lit unless you begged it desperately. Then he found her silverware drawer and set the table without asking. Granted, it wasn't challenging to find anyone's silverware drawer, but for a man to make himself useful without praising him every thirty seconds? It was spooky.

There had to be a catch.

"What do you usually drink for dinner? Wine, water, what?"

"You can have wine if you want. I know I've got a couple open bottles on the second shelf—not fancy quality, but okay. For myself, though, this day has been too much of a blinger to do wine."

He grinned. The smile transformed his face, whipped off five years and made her think what a hellion he must have been as a little boy. "So you'd like to drink…?"

"Long Island iced tea," she said primly.

He burst out laughing. "I got it now. Cut straight to the hard stuff."

"It's been an exhausting day," she defended.

"You're not kidding."

The phone rang yet again—it was just another call, nothing that affected life or death—so after that she turned down the volume and let the answering machine pick up. She wasn't ready to fix the sun and the moon, but she *was* prepared to concentrate on the lavender deal.

Still, the instant they sat down to dinner, it was obvious they wouldn't be talking business for a bit longer. "You haven't eaten in days?" she inquired tactfully.

"Not real food. Not food someone's actually taken the time to make from scratch." It was impossible to eat her spicy shrimp without licking one's fingers. But when he licked his, he also met her eyes. "Would you marry me?"

She rolled her eyes. "I'll bet you say that to all the girls."

"Actually, I never say it. I figured out, from a very short, very bad marriage years ago, that I'm too footloose to be the marrying kind. But I'm more than willing to make an exception for you.''

''Well, thanks so much,'' she said kindly, ''but I'd only say yes to my worst enemy, and I don't know you well enough to be sure you could ever get on that list.''

He'd clearly been teasing, but now he hesitated, his eyes narrowing speculatively. He even stopped eating—for fifteen seconds at least. ''That's an interesting thing to say. You think you'd be so hard to be married to?''

''I don't think. I know.'' She hadn't meant to sidetrack down a serious road. It was his fault. Once he'd implied that he wasn't in the marriage market, she instinctively seemed to relax more. Now, though, she steered quickly back to lighter teasing. ''Never mind that. The point is that you might want to be careful making rash offers like that, at least until you know the woman a little better.''

''Normally, yeah. But in your case I know everything I need to know. I haven't had food like this since…hell. Maybe since never. Where the hell did you learn to cook?''

''My mom. Most of her family was French, and she loved to putter in the kitchen, let all three of us girls putter with her. My one older sister is downright fabulous. Give Daisy a grain of salt, and I swear she can make something of it. Me, though…I just like to mess around with food.''

"Well, I can cook okay. I even like to—when I've got a kitchen to play around in. But at my best, I never came up with dishes like this."

That was enough compliments. The cats were circling, which he didn't seem to mind. She'd never fed them from the table, but that didn't mean anything. Telling a cat not to do something was like waving a red flag in front of a bull, and they'd all smelled the shrimp cooking.

Outside, evening was coming on. The crickets hadn't started up yet, but the birds had already quieted, the last of the day's sultry wind died down. It was that pre-dusk time when a soft, intimate yellow haze settled a gentle blanket on everything.

He'd leveled one plate, filled another. She had no choice about piling on more food. God knew how the man stayed so lean, but it was obvious he'd been starved. He even ate her asparagus soup with gusto, and that took guts for a guy.

"I didn't see that much, driving up—but it looks like you've got a beautiful piece of land here," he remarked.

"It is. Been in my family since the 1700s. My dad's side was from Scotland. Lots of people with that background here. Maybe they felt at home with the rocky land and the slopes and the stern winters." She asked, "Sometimes I catch a little French accent when you talk…which I guess is obvious if you work at Jeunnesse. But it's not there all the time. Do you actually live in France?''

''Yes and no. I've worked for Jeunnesse for better than fifteen years now. I like them, like the work. But basically what I've always loved is traveling around the globe. So I've got a small apartment in Provence, but I've kept my American citizenship, have a cottage in upstate New York. Both are only places I hang my hat. I live for months at a time wherever Jeunnesse sends me.''

''So there's no place you really call home?''

''Nope. I think I was just born rootless.'' He said it as if wanting to make sure she really heard him. ''You're the opposite, aren't you? Everything in your family's land is about people who value roots.''

''Yes.'' She suspected women had chased him, hoping they'd be the one who could turn him around. It was so ironic. She was as root bound as a woman could be. All she'd ever wanted in life was a man to love and a house full of kids. Still, discovering they were such opposites reassured her totally that nothing personal was likely to happen between them. ''You've never had a hunger for kids?'' she asked him.

''I've got kids. Two daughters, Miranda and Kate.'' He leaned over and filled her glass. She wasn't sure whether she'd finished two or he just kept topping off her first one. Either way she knew she wouldn't normally be prying into a stranger's life without the help of some Long Island iced tea. "My ex-wife still lives in upstate New York—which is why I've kept a cottage up there—so that I can easily come back a few times a year to see the girls. Although, often enough as they've gotten older, they've come to see me. They didn't mind having a dad spring for tickets to Paris or Buenos Aires."

"But didn't you mind missing a lot of their growing-up years?"

He got up and served the grape sorbet—once he'd determined that was the one course he hadn't tried yet. "Yeah. I missed it. But I tried the suit-and-tie kind of life when I was married. Almost went out of my mind. She kicked me out, told me I was the most irresponsible son of a gun she'd ever laid eyes on. But I wasn't."

"No?"

"No. I never missed a day's work, never failed to bring home a paycheck. It was sitting still I couldn't handle. Everyone can't like the same music, you know?"

She knew, but she also suspected there had to be some kind of story in those lake-blue eyes. Maybe he was a vagabond, one of those guys who couldn't stand to be tied down. But maybe something had made him that way.

She stood up and hefted their plates. His life wasn't her business, of course, or ever likely to be.

"I'll pop the dishes in the dishwasher, and then we can talk outside."

"Nope." He stood up, too. "I'll pop the dishes in the dishwasher, and you can put your foot up outside."

She let him.

Once he called out, "Is it okay if I put the cats in the dishwasher, too?"

And she yelled back, "Why, sure. If you don't want to live until morning."

He banged around in there, whistling something that sounded like "Hard-Hearted Woman," occasionally scolding the cats, but eventually he finished up and pushed through the back screen door, carrying another pitcher, sweating cold and jammed with ice cubes.

She'd already settled on the old slatted swing, with her sore foot perched on the swing arm and her good foot braced against the porch rail to keep the swing moving at a lullaby speed. He took the white wicker rocker and poured two glasses. "Two iced teas. No alcohol involved."

"Good." It was time they talked seriously. She knew it as well as he did, but the screen door suddenly opened as if by a ghost hand, startling them both...only to see a flat-faced golden Persian nuzzle her way outside. As soon as Cameron settled back in the rocker, the thug-size cat leaped on his lap.

"Could you tell your damn cat it's hotter than

blazes, and I need a fur coat on my lap like I need poison ivy?''

"It's hard to hear over her purring, but honestly, if she's in your way, just put her down.''

"Get down,'' he told the cat, in a lover's croon. But that wasn't the voice he used with her. Maybe he was stroking the cat, but the eyes that met hers had turned cool and careful. ''You think we've spent enough time getting comfortable with each other?''

"Enough to talk,'' she agreed, and settled one thing right off the bat. ''You've spent hours traveling and it's too late now to find a place in White Hills. You can stay here tonight, no matter how we work out everything else.''

"I'll camp outside,'' he said.

"Fine.'' ·She wasn't making a big deal out of where he hung his hat. He'd won some trust from her. Not a ton. But if she didn't feel precisely *safe* around him, it wasn't because she feared he was a serial killer or criminal. The man had more character in his jaw bone than most men did in their whole bodies. ''But it's your plan for my lavender that I want to hear about.''

"Okay. Then let's start back at the beginning. Apparently you've been developing some strains of lavender in your greenhouse. And over a year ago, you sent your sister Daisy a sample of a lavender you particularly liked.''

"I remember all that. I also remember her telling me that she'd passed it on to someone at Jeunnesse."

"That was me. And initially I thought your sister was the grower. That's why I talked directly with her instead of you."

Violet sighed in exasperation. "Honestly, Daisy wouldn't have deliberately lied to you. She's just had this thing about protecting me ever since I got divorced. So she probably just tried to keep me out of it until she was sure something good could come from a meeting."

"Well, the point is...you've been crossbreeding a variety of lavender strains and come up with several of your own."

"Yes," she concurred.

"Well, Jeunnesse has been making perfume for over a hundred years. They have thousands of acres of lavender under contract. You know the history? Provence was always known for its acres of lavender. It's breathtaking in the spring and summer, nothing like it on the planet."

Violet nodded. "I saw it twice as a girl. Our mom's family was from that area. We still have cousins there, and Mom always, always grew some lavender in the backyard to remind her of home. That's how I got my ideas to develop different strains."

Fluffball—her biggest cat, and the one with the brazen-honky-tonk-woman character—draped over his lap and exposed her entire belly for his long, slow stroking fingers. "Maybe you did it for fun, but it's more than fun to Jeunnesse. The lavender ground around Provence has become problematic for the perfume growers. It's not a matter of depleted soil or anything like that, because you can always add or subtract nutrients from a soil. But nematodes and diseases build up when the same crop is grown year after year, decade after decade. So now the company seeks to acquire long-term contracts with people across the world who have the right growing situation for lavender."

Before he could continue the educational lecture, she lifted a finger to interrupt. "Cameron. You don't have to talk to me as if I were quite that dumb. I know most of this," she said impatiently.

For a second she forgot how hard she'd worked to give him the impression she was a dotty flake, but he continued without a blink. "Then you also know that lavender isn't hard to grow. It doesn't need the pampering that lots of plants require. There are also already hundreds of strains of lavender across Europe and America and South America."

She knew that, too, but this time she didn't dare interrupt.

"So...now you come to my role in this. I'm one of Jeunnesse's agricultural chemists. What that amounts to is that I have a fancy degree that gives me a chance to travel and get my hands dirty at the same time. My job is to study new lavender strains. To evaluate how they work in a perfume equation. In fact, it literally took months for our lab to complete an analysis of the lavender you sent.''

''And—''

''And it's incomparable. It's sturdy. It's strong. The scent is strong and true, hardy. But more than all the growing characteristics I could test, your strain of lavender has the magic.''

''The magic?''

Cameron lifted his hands—annoying the cat when he stopped petting her. ''I don't know how else to explain it. There's a certain chemical ingredient and reaction in lavender that makes it critical to the fine perfumes. It's not the lavender smell that's so important. It's how the lavender works chemically with the other ingredients. To say it simplistically, I'd call it 'staying power.' And I can explain that to you in more depth another time. The point is that your lavender has it. We think. I think.''

She'd never grown the strains of lavender for profit. Or for a crop. Or for its perfume potential. She'd started puttering in the green houses after her divorce, when she'd first come home and had nowhere to go with all the anger, all the loss. Growing things had been renewing. But hearing Cameron talk, seeing the sunset glow on his face, feeling his steady, dark eyes as night came on, invoked a shiver of excitement and interest she'd never expected. "All right."

"Initially, Jeunnesse just wants to buy your crop. However you planned to harvest it, I'll either take charge or work alongside you, whichever you want. Obviously, your twenty acres are no big deal in themselves, it takes five hundred pounds of flowers to make an ounce of lavender oil. But I can easily get enough to analyze the quality and nature and characteristics of your lavender. Enough for me to extract some oil, my own way, under my own control, so we'll know for sure what we could have."

She'd stopped rocking. Stopped nursing her bee-stung foot. In fact, she'd completely forgotten about her bee-stung foot. "And then what happens?"

"Then, at the end of the harvest, we make some decisions. If your strain is as unique as I think it is, you have several choices. No matter what, you want to get started on patenting your strain. Then, if you want to grow it yourself—and can buy or rent the acreage to do it—then Jeunnesse would offer you a long-term contract. Another choice would be for you to sell the rights to Jeunnesse for a period of years. We're talking a long-term commitment, worth a great deal of money on both sides—that is, assuming your strain of lavender lives up to its potential. But we have to see what this mysterious strain of yours can do before making any promises."

Violet wasn't asking for promises—from him,

from Jeunnesse. When it came down to it, she wasn't asking for any promises from anyone anymore. She'd stopped believing in luck—or that anyone would be there for her—the day she'd caught Simpson in bed with his fertile little bimbo.

Now, though, she felt old, rusty emotions trying to emerge from her heart's cobwebs. For the lavender, she thought. It's not that she really believed she was suddenly going to get ridiculously lucky over something so chancy as her playing around in the greenhouse. It was just that there was no reason not to go along with Cameron's plan. Whether she got rich or not didn't matter. She had nothing to lose—and a lot of fun and interest to be had—just to see if this crazy thing came true.

For the lavender, she'd take a chance.

Not for the man.

But then, she'd never thought for a minute that Cameron Lachlan was a threat to her heart, so that wasn't even worth a millisecond's worry.

Four

The moonless night was silent as a promise. Cameron lay on his back on the open sleeping bag, trying to fathom why he felt so strangely moody and restless. He wasn't remotely moody by nature. Normally he'd have inhaled a special night like this. Clouds were building, stealing in from the west, concealing the moon but also bringing tufts of cooler air. God knew he was tired, and when he closed his eyes he could smell the sweet summer grass, the lavender in the distance, the blooms whispering out of Violet's garden.

The lights had gone off in the upstairs bedroom an hour ago. Vi had told him he could sleep inside—in the spare room, on the living room couch, on the porch, wherever he wanted. But Cam had sensed she was uncertain around him. If sleeping outside might make her feel safer, it was sure no hardship for him.

Any other time, he'd have treasured the night. He'd found some wild mint growing near her mailbox, rubbed it on his neck and arms, enough to chase off the mosquitoes and bugs. No dew tonight, so the grass was warm and dry. He heard the hoot of a barn owl, the cry of crickets. Fireflies danced as if Violet's long lawn were their personal ballroom.

He owned the world on nights like this—or that's how he'd always felt before. Instead the frown on his forehead seemed glued there. It made no sense. He loved his freedom, loved the smells and scents of a night this breathless, this private. He'd never been prey to loneliness. Something just seemed off with him lately. Especially tonight.

After Violet had gone inside, he'd walked all over her family farm. She had a pretty piece of land—but he'd seen pretty pieces of land before and never felt inclined to plunk down roots.

Cameron had long realized he had an allergy to roots, or any other possessions that could tie him down. His father had built up millions, running a company that—as far as Cam was concerned—had taken over his dad's life. Peter Lachlan had died before the age of fifty-five, with a son who never knew him, a wife who'd slept alone most of their marriage and fabulous possessions that didn't do much more than collect dust. Even as a young boy, Cameron had refused to follow in his father's footsteps. He'd carved his own, and if his independence and vagabond ways weren't everyone's choice, he'd loved his life.

It was just tonight that a weird, unsettled restlessness seemed to hem his mood, nipping at his consciousness, stealing his peace.

A sudden brisk wind brushed his hair. The cats, who'd been purring relentlessly at his side, stood up and shot toward the house. The black sky suddenly started moving, clouds being whipped like cake batter. The fireflies disappeared.

He felt the first drop of rain, didn't move. If the sky got serious, he'd move onto the porch, but it was still warmish. If anything, the sudden spin of damp wind brought out her farm's sweet scents. He told himself he was looking at the old red barn with the Dutch shingled roof, the rock fence, the rolling slope in front of him. But somehow his gaze kept straying to her house. Not the architecture of the sturdy old white farmhouse…but the shiny windows on the second story.

Specifically the window on the east. The one where the light had been switched off an hour before. The one with the filmy drift of white curtain at sill level. The one where he'd seen her unbraid that long, long pale hair and shake it free. The one where she'd reached behind her to unbutton her blouse—and then, damnation, disappeared from sight to take the rest of her clothes off.

He couldn't figure her out.

She was awfully bright for a batty woman.

She cooked better than a professional chef. Had more business pots going—the land, the house, the greenhouses, her herb and flower business—than any one person could normally take care of. She seemed to be emotionally and financially thriving on all that chaos, even if she did choose to dress like an old-fashioned spinster. She also seemed to make a point of acting as if she were witless, goofy, one of those fragile women who'd swoon if life put any stress on them.

As far as he could tell, she loved stress.

Most confusing of all, though, those soft eyes were studying him—then shying away—as if she were a young girl unfamiliar with the chemical pull between the sexes. She'd been married, for heaven's sakes. She'd surely had a hundred men react to her before. Besides which, he knew perfectly well when he sent off interested signals to a woman.

He *was* interested. Hell, she was sensual to her fingertips, complicated in personality and character, and he'd always liked complicated woman. But he needed to seriously work with her, and the instant they met, he picked up her wariness of him. So he'd sent out no signals, no vibes. He *knew* he hadn't. And he sure as hell wouldn't go near a woman when she made it clear she wasn't in the market for attention—at least not from him.

But damn. She was a handful of fascination.

Another raindrop plopped on his forehead. Then another.

From one breath to the next, a meandering drizzle suddenly turned into a noisy deluge. Skinny needles pelted down, warm and wet. He climbed to his feet quickly enough, but before he could scoop up the sleeping bag, he heard a warning growl of thunder...followed by a breathtaking crack of lightning that seemed to split open the sky.

Abruptly her back screen door slammed open. ''Damn it! Get in here!''

For a second he had to grin, lightning or no lightning. Unquestionably the screech came from his delicate flower of a hostess. The one with the vintage clothes and the fluttery hands who made out as if stringing a whole thought in a single sentence was a difficult challenge for her.

A yard light slapped on. Ms. Violet—harridan—Campbell showed up on the porch steps, barefoot, her tank and boxer shorts looking distinctly unvintage-like. In fact, her boobs looked poured into that tank, making him pause for another moment in sheer respectful appreciation.

''Have you lost your mind? That's lightning, for God's sake! Didn't you hear the storm coming? I kept waiting and waiting for you to come inside, but obviously you've been living in France too long. In America, we know enough to get out of the rain.''

"I'm coming—"

"By the time you get around to coming in, we'll both be electrocuted. Look. I may not have welcomed the idea of your sleeping in the house—for God's sake, I don't *know* you. But a storm is a storm, for Pete's sake.

"Pete's sake, God's sake… I'm getting confused whose sake is involved here—"

"Lachlan! Move your butt!"

Well, he'd been planning on it, but while she was screaming at him, she was also getting rained on. Which meant that tank and boxers were getting wet. And so was that long silvery curtain of blond hair.

Maybe he was thirty-seven, but he hoped to hell he never got so mature he failed to appreciate a beautiful woman. Particularly a beautiful woman whose attributes were outlined delectably between the yard light and the rain and the lightning.

On the other hand, being electrocuted posed a threat to his long-term ability to appreciate much of anything, so he hustled to the door just behind her. The instant she opened the screen, four cats seemed to leap from nowhere, determined to cut inline. And then, in the blink of a second, her yard light went out.

"There goes the power," she muttered.

It was his instinct to take charge, especially when a woman was in trouble. He couldn't help it. It was how he'd been raised—not by his absentee father, but by his mom, who'd expected even small kids to step up when there was a problem. He'd never minded. He liked stepping up. But in this case, the image Violet projected of being scatterbrained and helpless was—he was coming to understand—totally misleading.

She moved around in the dark, apparently gathering up candles—not the pretty decorative candles she had strewn all over the place but the practical, no-drippers she apparently stashed for no-power circumstances like this.

The back door opened off her kitchen, where she lit two and put them on the oak table, then kept going. She put one lit candle into a hurricane lamp, placing it in the bathroom off the kitchen, then carried more into the living room.

The living room, he'd noticed before, seemed to be part of the original farmhouse. In the dark, a guy could kill himself on all the stuff, but basically it was one of those long narrow rooms, with long narrow windows, requiring a long narrow couch. She'd done it all in roses and pinks—in case anyone could conceivably doubt she was female to the bone. Wade past the estrogen, though, and there was a massive old-fashioned brick hearth—big enough to roast a boar or two—where she lit four more candles.

"Better?" she asked.

"Can practically see well enough to read," he said mildly, although that wasn't exactly true. No matter how many fat white candles she lit, they didn't lighten the shadows. Mostly they lit up her. Eyes darker than secrets flashed up to his face, but he didn't think she really noticed him. She was too frazzled to think. Too frazzled to notice how that damp, stretchy red tank top was cupping her breasts.

"I can't guarantee we'll have light or water before morning," she said unhappily.

"Well, hell. I expected you to shut off that storm and restore the power immediately. What's wrong with you?"

He'd thought to lighten her up. It didn't seem to work. "I mean...I'm not sure the toilets will work."

"Inconvenient for sure, but more for you than me. If I have to step behind a tree before morning, I can probably cope."

"I'm afraid there's no phone."

"Damn. There goes another opportunity to make friends by calling people after midnight."

"*Lachlan.* Would you quit being so damn nice!"

He didn't get it. She seemed to be chasing around, lighting more candles for no particular reason that he could fathom. It was the middle of the night. So there was a storm. It was a sturdy house, nothing threatened by a little thunder and lightning.

And accusing him of being nice was a low blow.

No self-respecting male liked to think of himself as "nice." Yeah, he'd offered to sleep outside and made a point of communicating that he was a here-today-gone-tomorrow kind of guy, but that was just so she wouldn't be afraid of his coming on to her. It wasn't because he wanted her to think he was *nice*. Sheesh, how insulting could she get?

"You want me to drive into town? Is that why you're upset, because you feel stuck with me under your roof?" he asked. "There's just no reason to get your liver in an uproar. If I'm a problem for you, I'll just take off, go find a hotel or motel—"

"Oh, don't be ridiculous," she said crossly. "You're not taking off cross-country in the middle of the night in a thunderstorm. I never heard of anything so stupid."

Well, hell. Somehow he had to find some way to communicate with her a hell of a lot better than they were doing so far. They hadn't even started to do serious business, yet he seemed to invoke some kind of strange response from her. She was running on froth and emotional fumes. He needed her straight and coherent.

So he snagged her arm when she tried to go flying by—God knew where she was sprinting off to this time, but apparently her goal was to find more candles, even though the living room already looked like a witch's lair. She went stark still the instant his hand closed on her wrist.

"What are you doing?" she asked. She didn't shout it. Or whisper. Only...asked.

He felt her pulse gallop. Felt the warmth of her skin. Felt her gaze shoot to his face as if compelled by their sudden closeness. "I'm confused what's going on here. Are you afraid of storms?"

"No. Heavens. I grew up here. We get blizzards in winter, thunderstorms in summer. Vermonters are sturdy people. Actually, I love the rain."

Typical for her, she offered a lot of talk but very little information. "So it's just me, then? I'm doing something to make you nervous?"

"I'm not nervous. I'm always goofy," she assured him. "Ask anyone."

He struggled not to laugh. If he'd laughed, of course, she would have diverted him from the problem. Which made him wonder if that was why she came across so scatterbrained—because it was such an effective defense for her. "I don't want to ask 'anyone.' You're right here, I'm asking you. If you want me out of here, I'll leave. Just say the word."

She still hadn't seemed to breathe, although his hand had immediately dropped from her wrist. "You're staying. As long as you don't mind staying with a batty woman."

"You're not batty."

"You don't know me. I know me. And if I say I'm batty, I should know."

God. It was like trying to reason with a cotton

puff. Only she wasn't a cotton puff. In all that flickering candlelight her hair was drying, looking like silky silver. The pulse in her throat was beating hard. Her skin, her mouth, defined softness. And her eyes…she was still meeting his eyes. There was nothing goofy there, just the awareness between a man and a woman that carried enough heat to melt the Arctic.

He had no intention of kissing her. Maybe she was just figuring out the chemistry, but he'd known it since he first laid eyes on her. There was no explaining what drew a man and woman together—particularly when the two people were as contrarily opposite as they seemed to be—but Cameron didn't sweat problems he couldn't solve. When there was heat, there was heat. You didn't lie about it. You didn't pretend. You just faced the truth, whatever it was.

And the truth was, he didn't care if there was a combustible furnace of chemistry between them, he wasn't going to kiss her.

Yet suddenly he was.

He wanted to blame it on the moonlight…only there was none. In the dark candlelit room, with the growl of thunder and hiss of rain just outside, there seemed nothing alive but her and him. Nothing he could smell but her soft skin, the flower scents drifting from her hair, her throat. Nothing he could hear but the pounding of his own heart, in anticipation.

He didn't exactly remember how he reached for her, how his hands happened to curve on the swell of her shoulders, slide down, slide around her back to pull her into him. Yet he knew the exact moment, the exact sensation, when her hands reached up to lock behind his neck.

He could have sworn she'd been sending him keep-off, no-trespassing messages—yet if she didn't want to be kissed, she sure acted as if she did. Her arms swooped around his neck and she came up on tiptoe.

There was one more brief millisecond when he remembered all the reasons why this was a bad idea, but once she was that close, all rational bets were off. In a blink his mind turned to mush. Electric, excited mush.

He hadn't kissed anyone in a while. He hadn't kissed a woman this way in years. Hadn't wanted to. He thought it was long gone from his life, from his heart—that pull, that wonder, that wildness. He didn't know why it had to be her, didn't care.

She tasted like magic. Sweet, soft, alluring. Unforgettable. That pale-blond hair sifted through his fingers. Her head tilted back, accepting his kiss, inviting more than the graze of his mouth. Her lips asked to be taken. He answered.

One tentative kiss melted into another stronger one, another richer one, and then another that lost all track of time and space. His tongue found hers. Her heartbeat was suddenly racing, chasing, against his. Her arms nested tighter around his neck, and his hands molded down her spine, down to her fanny, pulling her closer to him.

Silver rain shivered down. Candles flickered. Shadows whispered of loneliness and old hurts and need. She'd been hurt. She'd been lonely. She needed. And maybe those were secrets she never meant to reveal to a stranger, but she didn't tell him anything. She just kissed him back, wildly, freely, intimately.

Cameron thought he was a man who took gutsy risks...but she was the brave one, the honest one, revealing so much. Something in her called him. Something in him answered her with a huge, nameless well of feeling that he'd never known he had.

He raised his head suddenly, feeling shocked and disoriented and unsettled. Her eyes were still closed, lashes lying like kitten whiskers on her cheeks, but when she finally looked at him, her eyes were luminous and her mouth wet and trembly.

"I never meant..." he started to say.

She gulped in a breath. "It's all right. I didn't think you did."

"It was the storm."

"I know."

"It was the moonlight."

"I know."

"I *need* you to know you can trust me. The last

thing in hell I wanted was to make you worried I'd—''

''I'm not worried. I'm thirty-four, Cameron. Too old to trust someone I barely know. But also way too old to make more of a kiss than what it was.''

''You said it exactly. That was just a kiss.'' He added, ''Right?''

''Right,'' she said firmly. ''We'll just mark this down as a moment's madness and forget all about it.''

Five

Violet's bedside telephone rang just after five in the morning. She jolted awake like a kicked colt. Mental images of her mom and dad or her sisters in an accident flashed through her mind in a panic as she fumbled for the phone. No one called this early unless there was a dire emergency—or unless someone had the sensitivity of an ox.

She clapped the receiver to her ear and recognized Simpson's voice.

Her pulse climbed back down from the worry stratosphere. Her ex-husband—like PMS and rain—could always be counted on to show up at the most inconvenient time. "Insensitive" should have been his middle name.

"Were you asleep?" he asked, his tone warmly ebullient.

"Me? Heavens, no." Why tell the truth? He wasn't worth it.

"Good. Because I didn't want to wake you. I just couldn't seem to resist calling. Vi, Livie had the baby."

As if someone slapped her, Violet instinctively braced against the headboard. "Congratulations."

"A son this time. We're going to name him John Edward, but Livie wants to call him Ed, after me."

"You got your son," she said.

"Yeah." Pride colored his booming baritone—pride that he'd never felt for her. Or with her. "Almost nine pounds. Twenty-two inches."

"He'll be playing football before you know it."

"Yeah, in fact—"

"I hope Livie's okay, and I'm happy you've got a son, Ed." She hung up, plunking down the receiver before he had a chance to continue the conversation.

For a second she had the oddest trouble catching her breath. The east window was open, letting in cool, rain-freshed air. Outside, nothing stirred in the pre-dawn light. Even the bugs were still snoozing. The sky was paler than smoke, the sunrise nothing more than a promise this early, but last night's violent storm had completely washed away.

Remembering the storm made her also remember how soundly she'd been dreaming until the telephone call. The dream pictures were still vivid in her mind…images of tumultuous kisses from a Scotsman named Lachlan, backdropped by Scottish lakes and moors and mist, her running naked and uninhibited through a moss-carpeted forest and Lachlan catching her.

The call from her ex-husband had certainly wilted *that* dream.

She pushed away the sheet and stood up, not awake yet—or wanting to be—but knowing she didn't have a prayer of going back to sleep. Not after *that* call. She tiptoed around the room, gathering clothes, not turning on a light, not wanting to wake Cameron down the hall.

It wasn't hard to navigate, even in the darkness. Unlike the rest of the house, which she'd jam-packed with girl stuff, she'd redone two of the upstairs bedrooms completely differently. One she'd turned into an office. For the other, her childhood bedroom, she'd bought a Shaker bed and dresser, painted the walls a virgin white, bought a plush white carpet, and called it quits.

Family and friends would find the decorating strange, she knew. All her life she'd gone for lots of color and oddball style and "stuff," yet, especially right after the divorce, the barren room suited her in ways she'd never tried to explain—not to friends, not even to family.

Now, though, the point was that she could easily

find her way around the room even in the dark…at least, if it wasn't for the cats tripping her. On the rare occasions she woke up this early, the cats usually ignored her and continued sleeping, but maybe they sensed how suddenly rattled she felt—possibly because of remembering Cameron's totally unexpected and very real kisses the night before. Possibly because of her ex-husband's call.

Ed hadn't called out of meanness. Violet had figured out a long time ago that Ed was far too unimaginative to be deliberately mean. He undoubtedly believed she'd want to know that his second child had been born, the son he'd wanted so much. No one knew more than Violet how much he'd wanted a son.

Downstairs, lights were on all over the place— she'd forgotten about losing power the night before. Forgotten almost everything when that sassy upstart Scotsman had pulled her into his arms.

She pulled on mud boots, a patchwork light jacket over her long denim skirt. Her hair was hanging in a wild heap down her back, but she didn't care. She needed…something. Air. A slap of morning. Some way, somehow, to catch her breath. She hadn't been all that upset about those kisses from Cameron until her ex had called.

Now, she felt all churned up. A young rabbit hopped across the grass, trying to evade her bodyguard contingent of cats—none of whom could catch road kill, they were all so fat and lazy, but the baby bunny didn't know that.

Violet aimed for the front door of the Herb Haven, then changed her mind and headed for the green-houses. There were two. The newest one she'd built herself, a couple years ago, but by this time in the summer, it was almost empty. Plants were all outside, either transported to the nursery or for sale in the business.

The original greenhouse, though, had been her mother's. It wasn't as high-tech as the new one, the heating and cooling and watering systems not even half as efficient. But her mom's sacred pruning shears were still hung on the wall, as was the old French apron she used to wear. Violet could remember the three sisters chasing up and down the aisles while Margaux potted and fussed with plants—her mom had always been the kind of mother who encouraged kids to get their hands dirty, to get *into* life, not just watch from the bleachers. Her sisters had often gone off with their dad into the fields. Not her.

She'd loved hanging out with her mom, loved watching Margaux nurturing and babying each flower, each herb, as if it alone were precious to her. She loved to dry the herbs, to watch her mom create artistic arrangements, to hear her mother insist that she needed to listen to each plant to understand what it needed. Her mom was a life lover, emotional about everything, an unrepentant romantic, a woman to the core. Margaux, in fact, was the only one who knew the real reason she'd divorced Simpson.

Of course, if Violet started remembering that ghastly memory, how Margaux had wrapped her up in a long, rocking hug and tried to soothe her like a child, she'd burst out crying. She didn't mind crying. She did it regularly, but it was just too darn early for that kind of heavy emotion, so she pushed up her sleeves and started puttering. In the heat of summer, there wasn't much left here in the greenhouse, either, but she still had some experiments going.

She plucked dry leaves, smelled the soil for health, and was just uncoiling a long skinny hose to mist-water her babies when she heard the door swing open. Cameron stood there, looking as devilish and sexy as he had the night before. In spite of the cool morning, his shirt was unbuttoned and he was wearing jeans so old and worn they cupped his bitsy butt and long, lean legs.

"Damn, did I wake you up? I tried to be quiet. After all your traveling, I figured you'd sleep most of the morning if you had a chance," she said.

"You didn't wake me up, but the phone did. A call that early usually means trouble. Everything okay?"

"Just hunky-dory," she said lightly. And then had to sniff fast. Tears welled in her eyes before she could possibly stop them—not that she would. When she was a young girl, she hated being so impulsive and emotional, but these days, she knew the power of it. Men got shook up when they saw tears. They backed away from an emotional woman. It all worked out fine. Usually.

"Hey." He saw the tears, and instead of looking frantic and freaked like any *normal* man, he walked slowly toward her. "What are we talking here? Bad news, bad morning, what?"

"An idiotic mood, that's all."

"Nobody died?"

"Nope."

"Some idiot dump you?"

"God, no."

"You hurt yourself? Another bee sting?"

"No. Nothing happened."

"Someone called," he persisted.

"Yeah. My ex-husband. To tell me that he and his wife had a baby. Their second. A son. They were very happy. And I'm very happy for them." Tears welled up again. Announcing her happiness and crying at the same time should *certainly* have ensured that Cameron thought she was a fruitcake.

Instead, as if unconcerned whether she made any sense or not, he ambled past her, squeezing her shoulder momentarily when he passed by. And then started snooping. Poking at her pots and plants. Sniffing. Tasting. Literally tasting.

How could she help but be diverted? "You usually eat dirt?"

"Yeah. I've tried every fancy chemical test known to man, but sometimes the senses seem to tell the most important truth. A taste'll tell me if the soil is highly acid or not." He moved on, doing more poking, more smelling, more snooping. "These are more of your lavender experiments?"

"Not just lavender." Because she was still feeling emotionally shaky, her tongue seemed to get loose. Not that her tongue needed an excuse to talk incessantly, but this time there was an actual reason. "Originally when I came home after the divorce, I didn't know what I wanted to do. Mom and Dad had retired south. This house was just left available for family. Dad wasn't ready to do anything else with it, thinking one of us girls could still want to live here. So it was perfect for me to move into...and I didn't have to rush getting a job, because I'd received a big settlement from the divorce. Partly there was a lot of money because he wanted the matrimonial house himself, and I didn't, so I got that share. But whatever. I thought of that settlement as guilt money."

"And was it?"

"Yeah. Big guilt on his part. But the point was, I came here and suddenly started remembering being a kid, trailing after my mom, all the pleasure we got out of growing things. Long term, I didn't have any idea what I was going to do for a career, but for a couple years the Herb Haven just hit me as right. A divorce is like...destroying something, you know?

So I wanted to create something. Grow things. Do something purposefully constructive instead of destructive.''

"You've got more than a green thumb," Cameron remarked.

"Yeah. It's kind of a joke in the family. Everything I touch seems to reproduce tenfold." Again she felt a round of tears threatening. "Come on," she said briskly. "I'll show you the lavender."

"First, I have to make you breakfast."

"Pardon?"

"Breakfast. You haven't had any. I haven't had any. And since you put me up, I'm cooking."

He made her crepes with blueberries. She sat at the table, lazy as a slug, letting him wait on her. It was another of the behaviors she'd taken up after Simpson—not kowtowing to men; acting like a spoiled princess. All normal men—certainly all Vermont men—steered way clear of an obviously high-maintenance woman, but Cameron...he just didn't seem to be normal.

If he remembered those potent kisses from the night before—or if they meant anything to him—he never let on.

If he found anything odd in a woman wearing dangling marquisite earrings and a patchwork jacket and rubber boots and uncombed hair, he never let on about that, either.

"I'm going to need a place to set up a minilab. If

I won't be in your way, I could use the potting room in your greenhouse—the old greenhouse we were in this morning. It seems perfect. It's got a sink and a longer counter for a work space, exactly what I need."

"It'll be too hot there," she said.

"I'm not afraid of heat."

"You'll get interrupted—"

"I can work around noise and interruptions."

"There's no comfortable chair. I can't make it into any kind of good working environment—"

"I don't need everything perfect. In fact, I'm usually bored by perfection. Life's a hell of a lot more interesting if we take the road less traveled, yes? Wasn't it a Vermont man who said that?"

Well, yes, but Robert Frost was safely dead, which Cameron certainly wasn't. In fact, although Cam was talking about his work…he kept looking at her. At her eyes. At her unkempt hair. At her bare mouth. As if he were communicating that he liked complicated women. Uncomfortable, difficult women. Hot women. As if he'd pegged her as less than perfect, the kind of woman who interested him.

"Well, do what you want," she said crossly. She glanced at the clock and abruptly stood up. "Thanks for breakfast, but I really have to go. I should have already opened my Herb Haven. I'll catch up with you later—"

She started to turn away when he suddenly said her name, very quietly, very gently.

"What?"

"I just want to make sure we're clear. You're okay with me working here. Living here. Setting up here for now."

"Sure," she said.

"We need to sign some agreements."

She motioned, an exasperated gesture. "I don't care about legal stuff like that."

"Yeah, you do. Because it's about potential money for you and protecting your rights."

"Well, I don't have time now." She took off, leaving him with the dishes and her house. Leaving him, surely, with the impression that she was flaky and emotional and not the kind of woman he'd want to be involved with.

He'd readily established that he wasn't looking for involvement. But those kisses last night—she didn't trust them. It seemed wise to make absolutely sure there was a five-mile fence of emotional distance established between them...so there'd be no more kisses.

Not just for his sake. For hers. Because a man like Cameron reminded her of everything she couldn't have.

Cam always had an unspoken impression that small towns in Vermont were quiet, bucolic, peaceful.

Violet's place was as peaceful as JFK International Airport on a holiday.

He made a quick trek to view her twenty acres of lavender, but he swiftly returned to the yard. He couldn't be that close to the lavender without making himself crazy. The field was breathtaking. She had plants close to harvest, florets already starting to open up, a few that were just days away from the perfect time to extract oil from and test. But he didn't feel right about touching the lavender until they'd both signed some legal agreements. Violet could trust him not to take advantage of her, but of course, she had no way to know that.

Sometime that day he simply had to trap her alone and sit on her until he'd made all the contract issues clear for her.

Until then, he figured he could spend the morning setting up. His gaze kept wandering around the yard and house and property as he unpacked his car and started carting equipment into the old greenhouse. It was odd. Normally he didn't much care where he was. Every place was new and interesting and involved different challenges. But there was something about her place—the land, the buildings, the whole feeling here—that provoked the strangest feeling.

He'd never been drawn to a place, partly because he'd always been bulldog stubborn about not becoming dependent on physical possessions. But damn. Some of the buildings showed wear and tear, the original house showed generations of character and age, but all of it looked well loved. The property kept striking him as a spot where a man could come and find a place for himself, feel as if he belonged.

Cam had never belonged anywhere. Never known he even wanted to. Of course, maybe his immune system was down and he was catching some annoying bug that was messing with his mind. He kept working.

Unfortunately, he always had to travel heavy. His clothes could be stuffed easily enough into a duffel bag, but he had to cart enough equipment to set up a minilab, and although he'd deny it to the death, he was just a wee bit fussy about his equipment. His microscope had cost a fortune—and was worth every penny, because his testing chemicals had to be exactly right. And he couldn't possibly carry around a full-scale distillation process, but he'd created a small, efficient steam distiller so that he could extract oil from small amounts of lavender.

Strangers assumed his old Birks and practical khakis meant that he was a totally laid-back personality. And he was. He'd been determined to convince himself for years that he was—except for his work, where Cam figured he had a reasonable excuse to be a perfectionist.

Setting up should have been a piece of cake after

doing it around the world all these years, but this morning, it seemed, one humorous problem followed another. To begin with, Violet's cats—for some God unknown reason—decided to hang with him. The old greenhouse had a lot of character, with a brick base and brick walkways and a nice, long concrete slab for a work space. But six of her mammoth, hairy cats sat on the greenhouse counter next to the sink, supervising every move he made. Worse yet, they wanted the water turned on. Regularly. Not a gush of water. A skinny little thread. And after one took her time getting a drink, it seemed the next one wanted her turn.

The herd of cats seemed to get thirsty about every twenty minutes.

By ten o'clock he hadn't accomplished much of anything. He suddenly looked up and noticed a girl leaning in the doorway. She was a young teenager, somewhere around fourteen, he guessed. She looked younger than spring grass, with eyes big as beacons, frothy brown hair and shorts two sizes too tight.

"Hi. I'm supposed to get some twine from in here." She motioned to the old cupboards above the sink.

"Go for it," he invited her.

But she didn't. She took a few steps in and then just kind of hung there, pulling her ear, changing feet, looking at the equipment he'd started to lay out. "I'm Boobla. Actually my name is Barbara and I'm sick to death of everyone calling me Boobla, but that's what my little brother called me when he was too little to say my whole name and then it stuck. I'm so sick of it, I could cry.''

"Okay. Barbara it is," he said obligingly.

"I work for Violet. Actually I'm her assistant manager.''

Cameron didn't raise his eyebrows, but this one was barely in a bra. It seemed mighty doubtful that she carried such a mighty title.

"I run the place when she's busy," Barbara offered further. "And Violet is really busy most of the time. We have tons of customers. And she's really nice, too. She said you were going to be here for a few weeks.''

"That's the plan.''

"Well, we're probably going to hire my friend Kari because we're so busy and all. But I'd still have time to help you. If you need anything, you could just yell in the shop for me.''

"That's really nice of you.'' He added carefully, "Barbara.''

"I like perfume and all. *Good* perfume," she qualified. "Not just the stuff you buy at discount stores. I've smelled the real stuff. We go shopping at Macy's every fall. Violet said you were a chemist. You had to go to college for a long time to do that, huh?''

Okay. So this morning he was doomed not to get

any work done. The kid eventually left, but cars and trucks zoomed in and out of the yard; he could hear the phone ringing both in Violet's house and the shop. Every time he carried something in from the car, someone else seemed to stop to talk to him. The mailman. A neighbor. A customer who assumed he'd know if Violet sold "Yerba mate", whatever that was.

He was annoyed, he told himself. He needed to get kicking, get serious, get into his job. But it seemed to be the kind of place where people took friendliness for granted. If you were in sight, you were fair game for conversation.

The sun poured down, heating up the day, making the cats want to snooze, bringing the irresistible scent of lavender wafting in from her east fields. Still, he tried to stay focused. Until he suddenly saw her striding out the back door of her Herb Haven, aiming for him.

Just like that, he felt a kick in the heart.

She was dressed just as goofy as the day before. Sandals today, paired with a sundress that wouldn't pass for work clothes anywhere he could imagine. The fabric was all sunflowers, matching long dangling sunflower earrings and a sunflower ring. She'd swished her long hair into a haphazard coil, to get the heat of it off her neck, he supposed, and her cheeks were flushed with heat and sunshine.

So were her eyes when she spotted him.

Or maybe the problem was his vision suddenly blurring when he spotted her. Those midnight kisses suddenly zoomed into his mind, sneakier than temptation, wilier than forbidden. Her mouth was naked this morning. Those same supple, plump lips asked to be kissed. Those same striking hazel eyes dared him to figure her out.

She was a complicated, contradictory woman, he told himself. There were a ton of signs that she was too much trouble. To begin with, she was obviously a home-and-hearth kind of female, which meant he had nothing in hell to offer her. And then there was the mystifying issue of how she could be so damned beautiful and yet totally unattached. On top of that, the woman acted like a complete flake sometimes and other times clearly had a tantalizing brain. Whatever secrets she was holding back, it seemed obvious that she didn't need a guy messing with her who wasn't serious. There was too much vulnerability in those huge eyes.

Too much vulnerability in those kisses.

Better that he should stay clear, knowing he was only going to be there for a short time.

"You have a few minutes, Cam? I can steal a half hour now, if you want to go look at the lavender."

"Ready," he said. But the minute she came close, he felt his world shift. It was nuts. He'd had tons of women shake his timbers and move his hormones. Her pulling his chain wasn't a new issue. He liked his chain pulled, for God's sake. But those eyes, that hair, that smile…

Be careful, his heart warned him.

Which was the craziest thing of all, because Cam never, never did uncareful things.

Six

Violet understood that she couldn't postpone dealing with the touchy lavender problem forever, but just then she was saved by the bell—or the ring, as it happened. Barbara yelled from the Herb Haven that there was an overseas telephone call for her. That meant Daisy had to be on the line—and there was no way she wanted to postpone a chance to talk with her sister.

She sent Cam up to the house for lunch. It was an easy way to get him out of listening range. Suggest food and men always moved. Once in her broom-closet-size office in the Herb Haven, she closed the door and listened to Daisy's perky greeting.

"So. He got there. What'd you think of him?"

Violet briefly held the phone away from her ear to stare at it, then clapped it back tight. "Wait a minute. What is this?"

"What's what?"

"You know what. What I think of *him* should have nothing to do with a lavender deal. His being here is supposed to be about oil. Lavender oil. And for the record, all the legal stuff sounds like a nightmare."

"It is," Daisy said cheerfully. "But don't worry about it. Just leave all that junk to Cam. He's straight as an arrow. With any luck, you're going to make a fortune, kiddo. And in the meantime, you'll have a chance to forget that bubble-brain you finally got divorced from."

Violet closed her eyes and prayed for patience. She loved both her sisters, even if both of them could be total pains. Camille was the youngest, though, so she was more easily suckered. If Violet wanted Camille to do something, she just nurtured and fed and mothered until Camille either gave in or begged for mercy. Getting Daisy to behave was a far tougher challenge.

Daisy was the beauty of the family. God knew how Mom had named her for the common flower, when she was the exotic tropical blossom of the clan, with a model's figure and that kind of style and élan. Daisy also had guts—enough guts to take off for France and live a wild, free lifestyle like everybody dreamed of but nobody ever really did. Unfortunately nobody could bully Daisy. Daisy could exhaust the whole family with her sneaky, take-charge, bossy ways.

"Something smells really, really rotten here," Violet said darkly. "How long have you been planning this? You didn't send Cameron Lachlan over here just for the lavender. You were thinking about setting me up. Damn it, you twerp. You didn't think I'd fall for Cameron, did you?"

"Come on. He's adorable."

"He's a lot of things, but adorable isn't one of them. Good-looking, yeah. Rough and tough, yeah. Independent, yeah. Great eyes, yeah. But adorable is a word for boys."

"Exactly. You don't need any more *boys* in your life. About time you had a man scale your walls."

"I beg your pardon."

"I don't know for sure what that bozo did to you, and neither does Camille. But we both know something was bad at the end. So, fine. Broken bones take six weeks in a cast. Broken hearts taken longer. But you were made to be married, Vi. It's time to take another chance."

"You're out of your mind. And I'm going to tell Mom you did this to me."

"Are you kidding? Mom's in on it."

"You're low. Lower than a skunk. Lower than an

earthworm. I thought you were my favorite sister, but not anymore.''

''Uh-huh.'' Daisy yawned through this threat. All three sisters regularly pulled the ''favorite sister'' jealousy thing on each other. But something happened then. As clear as the connection to France was, something seemed different—as if Daisy put her hand over the mouthpiece—and when she suddenly came back on, her voice changed. The real humor in her tone now sounded forced. ''Listen, you, it's your turn for some happiness. You don't have to tell me what happened before the divorce—''

''What's wrong?'' Violet said.

''Nothing's wrong.''

Violet wasn't the maternal sister for nothing. Her job in the family was to be the caretaker, the one who made chicken soup when the other two were dumped, the one who cleaned up their scrapes and listened to stuff they couldn't tell their mother. ''The last four times you've called, something hasn't been right in your voice. Is the romance fading with Monsieur Picasso? You tired of living in France?''

''What could be wrong? The romantic French countryside, a hot summer sun, bougainvillea outside my window, breezes off the Mediterranean, freedom, a country where men really know how to appreciate a woman—''

Now Violet started to get really worried. ''Quit with the horse spit. He hasn't hurt you, has he?''

"No. And quit turning the subject around. We're talking about you. You and love. You and sex. You and Cameron. Just think about it, would you? He's not the marrying kind. But he's a good man. The kind who'll be honest. And good to you. A good guy to get your feet wet in the love pool again, without having to make any major risky dives. Besides which, he really is an answer for your lavender problem."

When Violet hung up, she thought, what's wrong with me has nothing to do with lavender. And it can't be fixed.

She hustled to the house to grab some lunch—but there was no further serious talking with Cameron, because he was the one to get a phone call that time. One of his daughters kept his ear pinned for almost a half hour.

She was dying to ask him some questions about that conversation, but about the time he hung up, she saw the roofer's truck bounce into the yard. Par for the course, the roofers were late, so she ran over to the cottage to raise hell.

Just when she tried to track down Cameron again, the lady from the *White Hills Gazette* showed up with her sunny face and her legal pad—Violet remembered the interview, didn't she? No, she hadn't remembered, and she hadn't had time to put on lipstick in hours now, but publicity for the Herb Haven was too important to pass up.

An hour later, she glanced up to see Cameron in the doorway, listening to her rant on about the events and products and courses she'd scheduled for the summer. He lifted his hand in the air, showing her what looked to be an oatmeal raisin cookie. Thank God. If she didn't get some sugar and junk food soon, she was probably going to fade out altogether.

After the interview, she leveled the plate of cookies he'd brought—but he'd disappeared by then. She searched until she found him on her back porch, talking with Filbert Green.

Filbert was the farmer her father had hired to caretake the farm after her parents retired to Florida. The idea was for Filbert to put in corn and soybeans or whatever, to keep the land in shape, until one of the Campbell daughters realized how much they belonged on the Vermont homestead and settled down to have some kids.

Camille had just gotten married, but she had no need for the land, and heaven knew when or if Daisy was coming back from France. So when Violet had limped home after the divorce, the house had been empty and everyone happy she was going to stay there. She'd let Filbert go. She wanted to wallow on the land in peace and quiet. Now, though, she saw Filbert hunkered down on her porch with Cam hunkered down next to him, both of them drawing plans with sticks like two smudge-nosed boys in a sandbox. They were talking about her lavender. Talking about the harvest. What needed doing, who'd do it, how. She needed to listen, needed to actively participate, only, damnation if there wasn't another interruption.

Kari was the interruption, and actually it occurred to Violet by then that the girl had been shadowing her around for some time. A job interview, she recalled. Kari wanted a job, and God knew Violet was so behind she could barely catch her own tail. The girl was hardly out of diapers, but damn, she could talk spreadsheets like a true computer geek.

"Okay. These are the rules. Take 'em or leave 'em. I don't give a damn what you wear, as long as you don't show up naked. I don't care if you're late or early as long as the work gets done. But you have to like cats. And I need accurate records. I can't work with someone who's careless with numbers. So. Are we square or not?"

Kari of the shy smile and hopelessly baby blue eyes suddenly turned shrewd. "How much you gonna pay me?"

"How much you want?"

"Ten bucks an hour. I'm worth it."

"This is your first job. Don't you think that's a little high?"

"Beats me. That's what my dad told me to ask for, first try."

"Okay, then you got it, first try. I love guts in a girl."

Once she put the girl on the payroll, by a miracle, she caught a thirty-second break. In those thirty seconds, she remembered those kisses of Cameron's from last night, how she'd felt—how he'd felt—and whether she dared entertain the extraordinary fantasy of making love with him.

Cripes, it was one of those days when she could barely find time to pee, so considering a love affair seemed the height of lunacy. But her sister's phone call had helped promote the lunacy. Daisy had pointed out that Cameron had a uniquely perfect qualification for a lover—he didn't want to settle down.

For another woman, that would obviously be a disadvantage. But for her... For three years now, she'd been afraid of attracting a man who'd want a normal, married type of life with her. Cameron was the first guy where she was dead sure he wouldn't want something from her that she couldn't give.

On top of which, she couldn't even remember feeling this level of lust and longing for a man she'd barely met. There was something dangerous about that man. Something wicked. Something that made her dream about dumb things she knew she couldn't have.

Thankfully, the insane day just kept getting worse. There were no more thirty-second breaks. Around four, she gulped down two glasses of water before she keeled over from heat exhaustion, remembered she had a killer bee sting, babied it with some honey, then abruptly heard raised voices from inside the shop.

She hiked out to find Boobla near tears, being railed on by an unsatisfied customer. Wilhelmena wanted a cure for age. There wasn't one. It seemed she'd bought some chamomile and clover and mint and parsley and primrose a few weeks ago, believing the combination of products would clear up her wrinkles and fix her dry skin, and now she wanted a refund because they didn't work.

Violet gently stepped in front of her clerk. "Those are all good ideas for dry skin, but I don't know why you had the impression they'd fix wrinkles."

"Because your girl told me it would."

Violet didn't have to ask Boobla to know the teenager never said any such thing. "If you don't want the products, you can bring them back. I'll give you a partial refund."

"That isn't good enough."

Violet's gaze narrowed. She knew Wilhelmena. Hell's bells, every shopkeeper in three counties knew Wilhelmena. "I'm afraid you'll have to sue me then, hon, because that's as far as I'm going."

The woman railed a little while longer. For anyone else, she'd have gone the long mile, but not for a complainer—and then there was the principle of backing up her staff. Boobla was still a baby, which was precisely the point. This was her first job. Violet wasn't about to let anyone browbeat her just because she was a kid.

More customers came and went. In the meantime, orders for baskets still had to be filled, plants needed watering, the grass mowed. Even after hours, the phone kept ringing and a delivery truck came in.

The next time Violet looked up, somehow it was well past seven. The kids had both gone home, the closed sign was parked in the window, and Cameron was standing in the Herb Haven doorway with the fading sun behind him.

"What the hell kind of place are you running here, chère?" he murmured.

"What do you mean?"

"I mean you're doing the work of four men and then some. You barely had time to grab half a sandwich at lunch, and I know you had a couple of cookies. But have you had anything serious to eat since breakfast?"

Who knew? Who cared? She had no idea how long he'd been standing there, but the silence suddenly coiled around her nerves like velvet ribbons. He looked like such a shout of male next to all the flower sights and smells and fuss, especially with his leg cocked forward and his broad shoulders filling the doorway. When she met his gaze, there was no instant thunderclap, just more of those itchy-soft velvet nerves. She was just so aware that no one else was in sight or sound but her and Cam and all that golden dusk.

But then she recalled his question. He sounded as if he were accusing her of being an effective manager, so Violet instinctively defended herself. "I really don't work very hard. All my running around is just an act—to fool people into thinking I have a head for business. I'd be in real trouble if the customers ever realized I don't have a clue what I'm doing."

"Sure," Cam said, but there was a wicked glint in his eyes. She had a bad feeling he was on to her flutter-brained routine—which was a foolish fear, since every guy in the neighborhood and surrounding county had been convinced for years she was a hard-core ditz. He distracted her, though, when he lifted a white paper bag and shook it.

She smelled. "Food?"

"Don't get your hopes up. It's nothing like what you cook. But I made a trek into White Hills and picked up some fresh deli sandwiches, drinks, dessert. By midafternoon I figured that I'd never get you out to the lavender to talk unless I somehow wooed you away from the phone and the business. I thought you must be hungry by now."

She wasn't. Until she looked at him. And then realized there seemed to be something hollow inside her that had been aching for a long time.

"I don't have long," she said.

He nodded, as if expecting that answer, too—but shook the bag again, so she could catch the scent of a kosher dill and corned beef on rye.

"I don't usually eat red meat," she said twenty minutes later, as she was wolfing down her second sandwich.

"I can see you're not into it."

"And I never eat chips. They're terrible for you."

"Uh-huh," he said, as he opened the second bag of chips and spilled them onto a napkin.

She wasn't exactly sure how he'd conned her into this picnic, but he seemed to have pulled a Pied Piper routine—his carrying an old sheet to use as a table-cloth, and the food and his car keys and strapping her into the front seat and his driving—while she did nothing but follow the scent of food. By the time he'd unfurled the sheet to sit on, on the crest of the east hill overlooking the lavender, she'd already been diving in.

He had a kind side, she had to give him that, because he didn't say a word when she gobbled down the second helping of chips. All that salt. All that fat. She tasted guilt with every bite, but, man, were they good. "You really ate ahead of time?" she insisted again.

"Sure did," he said.

But she wasn't convinced. He'd brought enough for two. She'd assumed he was diving in when she was, until she suddenly glanced up and noticed that he was mounding his food on her plate. "I never eat this much. You must think I'm a greedy pig."

"Yeah. I've always admired greed in a woman. Always admired meanness, too, and you've got an unusually mean streak. I was watching how you treated those two kids who work for you. They both think you're a goddess."

"Are you making fun of me?"

"Are you kidding? I'm in awe, chère." When she finally finished enough to please him, he reopened the bag and emerged with more goodies. "Almond cookies. And there's a little more raspberry iced tea. Although I only bought a few cookies. I had no idea you were going to need three or four dozen just to fill you up on a first round."

The darn man was so comfortable and fun to be with that she had to laugh…but then, of course, reality caught up with her. She couldn't be feeling comfortable. Not here.

It wasn't that she never came out to this stretch of the farm. She'd planted the twenty acres of lavender over the past few years, after all. Still, she avoided this view if she could help it. She wasn't the one who'd tended it—her younger sister Camille had, when she'd come home early in the spring, yelling the whole time about how crazy Violet had become to neglect anything like this.

And the craziness was true. Obviously, she knew she was coming out here with Cameron; they had to

An Important Message from the Editors

Dear Reader,

Because you've chosen to read one of our fine romance novels, we'd like to say "thank you!" And, as a special way to thank you, we've selected two more of the books you love so well, plus an exciting Mystery Gift, to send you absolutely FREE!

Please enjoy them with our compliments...

Pam Powers

Peel off Seal and Place Inside...

EDITOR'S FREE GIFT SEAL THANK YOU

How to validate your Editor's
FREE GIFT
"Thank You"

1. Peel off gift seal from front cover. Place it in space provided at right. This automatically entitles you to receive 2 FREE BOOKS and a fabulous mystery gift.

2. Send back this card and you'll get 2 brand-new Silhouette Desire® novels. These books have a cover price of $4.25 each in the U.S. and $4.99 each in Canada, but they are yours to keep absolutely free.

3. There's no catch. You're under no obligation to buy anything. We charge nothing—ZERO—for your first shipment. And you don't have to make any minimum number of purchases—not even one!

4. The fact is, thousands of readers enjoy receiving their books by mail from the Silhouette Reader Service™. They enjoy the convenience of home delivery...they like getting the best new novels at discount prices BEFORE they're available in stores...and they love their *Heart to Heart* subscriber newsletter featuring author news, horoscopes, recipes, book reviews and much more!

5. We hope that after receiving your free books you'll want to remain a subscriber. But the choice is yours—to continue or cancel, any time at all! So why not take us up on our invitation, with no risk of any kind. You'll be glad you did!

6. Remember...just for validating your Editor's Free Gift Offer, we'll send you THREE gifts, *ABSOLUTELY FREE!*

GET A *Free* MYSTERY GIFT...

SURPRISE MYSTERY GIFT COULD BE YOURS **FREE** AS A SPECIAL "THANK YOU" FROM THE EDITORS OF SILHOUETTE

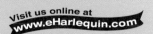

Visit us online at
www.eHarlequin.com

The Editor's "Thank You" Free Gifts Include:

- Two BRAND-NEW romance novels!
- An exciting mystery gift!

PLACE FREE GIFT SEAL HERE

Yes I have placed my Editor's "Thank You" seal in the space provided above. Please send me 2 free books and a fabulous Mystery Gift. I understand I am under no obligation to purchase any books, as explained on the back and on the opposite page.

326 SDL DZ6P   225 SDL DZ64

FIRST NAME	LAST NAME

ADDRESS

APT.#	CITY

STATE/PROV.	ZIP/POSTAL CODE

(S-D-06/04)

Thank You!

◄ DETACH AND MAIL CARD TODAY! ▼

The Silhouette Reader Service™ — Here's how it works:

If offer card is missing write to: The Silhouette Reader Service, 3010 Walden Ave., P.O. Box 1867, Buffalo, NY 14240-1867

BUSINESS REPLY MAIL

FIRST-CLASS MAIL   PERMIT NO. 717-003   BUFFALO, NY

POSTAGE WILL BE PAID BY ADDRESSEE

SILHOUETTE READER SERVICE
3010 WALDEN AVE
PO BOX 1867
BUFFALO NY 14240-9952

NO POSTAGE
NECESSARY
IF MAILED
IN THE
UNITED STATES

get the harvest business settled. But for whole long stretches of time, she forgot how traumatically symbolic the lavender was for her.

A knot filled her throat as she gazed at the stretching, rolling sweep of lavender. Until Camille had come home, the long rows of lavender bushes had been an unkempt, overgrown thatchy mess. They still weren't perfect, yet Violet—who had always nurtured and mothered everything and everyone—had thrown these plants in the ground and just left them.

Cameron suddenly said quietly, "Tell me what you originally planned to do with this?"

His voice was gentle, serious, nonjudgmental, but she couldn't speak for the lump in her throat—not for that moment.

The smell of lavender saturated the warm summer air. The buds were just barely coming on, because all the strains she'd put in were late types. Buds would keep coming from now through August, and by late summer the smell would be unbearable, invading everything, impossible to escape from—not that anyone would want to.

The plants were pale purple, soft in the evening light, and that first blush of bud smell was like nothing else—not at all heavy, but immeasurably light, a scent that was forever fresh and frisky and clean. There was nothing quite like it. No other flower, no other herb, had a scent even remotely related to lavender.

"Violet?"

When he prompted her, she motioned to the field without looking at him. "Our mom—her name was Margaux—always had lavender growing in the backyard. She's the one who taught me what I know. There are all kinds of lavender, but basically most strains fall in one of two camps. 'Hardy lavender' is what a lot of people call English lavender, even though it's not from England. And the 'tender lavenders' tend to grow around France and Spain."

Cameron leaned back. "Go on."

"Okay. The thing is…you get the finest oil—as far as perfume—from the hardy lavenders. Which I guess you obviously know, huh?"

"I may know just a little something about that, yeah. But keep talking, anyway. I want to know how you got into this, how you developed this strain."

There. She was starting to unchoke. Cameron surely knew all this stuff already if he was a chemist, but babbling was one of her best ways of covering up nerves. "Well…I knew from my mom that there are advantages to each type of lavender. The oil wasn't really my interest, because I already realized you needed some ridiculous amount—like 500 pounds of flowers—to get even ounces of the oil. But some lavenders are stronger in color and scent. Some are hardier as far as where they can grow."

She wasn't going to think about babies. She was just going to keep talking until she got a good grip and could look at Cameron with a smile again. "Anyway, after the divorce, I had time on my hands. And Daisy happened to send me some interesting strains of lavender, so then, for fun, I just started setting up some experiments in the greenhouse. I brought in some of my mom's favorite strains from her garden, then started collecting others from around the country. What I wanted to do was just... play...see if I could blend the best qualities of all my favorites."

"For what reason?" Cameron asked.

"Just for fun. Just to see if I could do it, if I could produce a lavender where the scent stayed truer than all the other types. I always loved puttering with plants, you know? And—" She stopped.

She was lying to him. Images spilled through her mind, mental pictures of the man she'd once married and believed was the love of her life. She'd learned everything she knew about sex from Simpson—particularly all the wrong things. Things like how guys needed to get off or they suffered. Things like how guys couldn't wait. Things like Real Women climaxed with no problem unless they were inhibited. Also, Real Women got pregnant as long as the guy was virile, and Simpson's sperm—he'd had that checked—were damn good swimmers.

She was the one with the skinny tubes.

"Violet, what's wrong?" Cameron asked quietly. She stared at the field until her eyes started to clear. "After the divorce...I just wanted to grow things. Reproduce things. Everybody thought I was crazy to let this field get so out of control. They were all right. But the truth, Cam, is that I didn't care if it was out of control."

"All right," he said.

"It was *mine* to love or lose. If I lost it, if I never made a dime, I didn't care. I don't need money from it. I can afford the loss. I don't really give a damn if anyone thinks I'm crazy or not."

"Hey," he said gently.

Tell him, her heart said. Just tell him. Then it's out on the table. You'll know if it's important to him or not.

But she knew it wasn't that simple. Cameron might have an already grown family; he might not want kids. But a lot of men thought a woman was less than a complete woman—less sexual, less feminine—if she was infertile.

"I just wanted to grow something. Of my own. I wanted to make something out of land that had been barren, because this slope was rocky and nothing ever grew well here before. So it was the challenge. To create something that hadn't existed before. It wasn't about making money. It was just about—"

"Whoa," Cameron whispered, and as if he had some cockamamie idea that he was dealing with a fragile woman on the verge of a big, noisy, crying jag, he swooped her into his arms.

Seven

The last thing Cameron intended to do was pull Violet into his arms.

Yeah, he'd dragged her off to the lavender field—and brought the picnic dinner—but that was only because he finally figured out the whole picture. Violet's herb business was chaotically busy. Unless he found some way to isolate her from the phone and her neighbors and all the other people noise, he figured they'd never get the contract details settled between them. That issue was critical. Even though the nature of her lavender strains were supposed to be harvested late, the huge heat wave was bringing on the crop at the speed of sound. Within days, they needed to start the harvest.

So he'd taken her to the one place where he knew he could talk to her privately, but not to seduce her. Not to even think about touching her. Nothing would have happened—Cameron really believed—if she hadn't suddenly looked so shaken up.

He couldn't stand it. Violet was so full of energy. For damn sure, she was a manipulative, confusing woman who seemed to mislead a guy about the truth of things. She was stubborn, independent to an exasperating degree, a woman who did exactly what she wanted on her own timetable. She was a tough cookie—even if for some reason she didn't want anyone to know it.

And that was exactly why it killed him to see her eyes fill up, suddenly so full of hurt and sadness. He'd *had* to grab her. He wasn't thinking of romance, he was just responding instinctively to a need to protect her, comfort her somehow.

Only a split second later, all his honest, sincere, chivalrous intentions went to hell.

The very instant his mouth came down on hers, the damn woman *responded.* Her lips were warm as sunshine, as soft as silver. Her head tipped back, willingly absorbing the pressure of his mouth and his first kiss…which gave him absolutely no choice but to follow through with a second kiss and then a third. Her eyelashes fluttered down and her slim fingers seemed to hesitate, then slowly climb his shoulders and curve around his neck.

When he felt her warm, supple body slide against his…something happened. Deep inside him, there was a silent whoosh, as if the rest of the world disappeared from sight, sound, touch. She was his reality. She, and all the senses she invoked.

He clutched her tighter. She clutched right back, and suddenly all that long, wild, silky hair was coming loose in his hands. Her bracelets jangled, one of her sandals slipped and tumbled down the slope; yet she never opened her eyes, never made out like there was a damn thing that mattered to her but him—and getting more of those sweet, dangerous, uninhibited kisses.

Maybe he was guilty of initiating that first kiss. Maybe he knew he shouldn't have, knew she was trouble. But how could he possibly, conceivably have guessed that she'd be *this* much trouble?

He'd tasted her before. It had been intense, but not like this. Whatever had shaken her seemed to act like some kind of trigger, as if something tight and trapped were suddenly freed from deep inside her. She not only kissed him back but dumped emotional rocket fuel on the flames. She didn't just yield but sought. She didn't just touch but invited, demanded, his touch.

Warm, damp skin slid against his. He smelled her hair, her ice-raspberry breath, the lick of scent on her skin. As the night dropped, with the moon showing up like a promise in the far sky, it seemed as if suddenly all those acres of lavender released a whole song of scent. The lavender flowed all around them, filling the air, filling their senses, teasing their sense of taste and smell. The scent was so like her—wild and fresh and elusive. Magical.

''Cam,'' she whispered, her voice barely a whisper, an ache of wonder.

He felt the same wonder, tried to steal more in another kiss. His hand drifted down, shimmering over her collarbone and then to her breast, snuggling there. No matter how carefully, how reverently he touched, his body groaned that it wasn't enough. Not nearly enough.

Her blouse pushed up, pushed off fairly easily.

For a second he thought she wasn't wearing a bra—but she was, it was just that the fabric was a teensy scrap of lace. A front opener, though, easy enough to unlatch. And then he had his warm callused hand on her immeasurably soft breast, the flesh swelling for him, the nipple perking under his palm—only that wasn't enough, either. Not even close to enough. She groaned against his mouth, so he bent down and delivered kisses down her throat, down to her breasts, faster kisses now, rougher ones.

Somewhere he still had a functioning conscience—a murky conscience, but one stabbing him with warning instincts. He knew he didn't understand her. Knew she had some troubling deep waters that she hid from sight. Knew she was a worrisome maze of contradictions.

He'd seen her supposed flaky side…yet he'd also seen how many balls she efficiently, effectively juggled, even on an average business day.

He'd also heard her claim more than once how she didn't care if the lavender had gotten out of control, yet that was impossibly contradictory, too, because no one accidentally experimented in a greenhouse to the tune of twenty acres of lavender.

And then there was her wildly estrogen-overdosed house, compared to that strange, contrary shock of her austere nun-like bedroom he'd only glimpsed.

He couldn't be sure of anything, not around her, except for the one obvious thing—that he was here for the lavender. And to do that business, they had to be able to trust each other. To seduce her before she could trust him was as foolhardy as betting on a lottery.

He'd never been foolhardy. Independent, yes. Self-centered, oh, yes. But never a fool.

"Cam," she whispered again, this time pleating his shirt open with her hands, pulling at it, reaching to touch his bare chest with her own.

His head promptly swelled with fool's thoughts, fool's needs, filled so full there was nothing else but her, her taste, her profile in the moonlight, her lavender-whispered skin, her winsome, demanding mouth.

He *had* to go back for more. This pull for her—he had to get a grasp of it. What he felt with her, for the land, for everything here was alien to the Cameron Lachlan he knew himself to be. He'd sworn never to become like his father, never to become attached to a place. He'd sworn never to let any place own him. Ever.

Yet there was something about her that made him feel this horrifying, embarrassing, stupid sense of belonging. She made him feel as if she needed him.

As if he needed her.

As if she wanted him—*just* him, not any man, not any guy, but only him.

He wanted her, only her—not just a woman to fill a sexual need or the lonely hours of the night, but something else, something more. Cameron kept getting the unnerving, frightening impression that he wanted her the way he'd wanted no other woman. That she alone could fill a hole inside him that he hadn't even known was there.

The night kept coming, bringing the privacy of darkness, intensifying the scents of verdant earth and lavender. The ache inside him felt part of the night, lonely and dark, hot and urgent. He knew it was crazy, yet the drumbeat of his pulse kept thrumming the same message, that he'd lose something irretrievable if he didn't love her, didn't have her, now, right now.

She lay back against the cool sheet he'd brought

as a picnic blanket, pulling him down to her, communicating how much she wanted the same thing. Him. Naked. Now. For whatever reasons, right or wrong, sane or crazy, this felt so right. *She* felt right.

His shirt peeled away as easily as her skirt. She made an exasperated sound, half sat up, peeled off a tangle of noisy jewelry from her wrists and ears, came back to him, damp soft skin intimately molding to his. He had to devour her with more kisses. Against the white sheet, her skin looked so golden dark, her eyes so shining, and all that wild silken hair kept tangling him closer. He thought she was naked, but it seemed she was still wearing see-through panties…panties he didn't discover until his mouth had trailed an intense, tender path from her breast to the hollow in her navel, down to the sweet roundness of her abdomen and finally lower.

Even in the dark, he could see through those filmy panties. Even in the dark, he could see the urgent rise and fall of her breasts, the pulse drumming in her throat, the heat in her eyes. And when those panties were gone, when there was nothing between them but anticipation, she said suddenly, wildly, "Cam… Cameron, I need to tell you something—"

"Birth control. You're not protected?"

For a millisecond she didn't answer, but then she said with absolute sureness, "No. That's not a problem."

"Then you'd better give me a very fast, very serious reason to stop, chère, or else I'm going to be very sure you want this as much as I do."

Again she hesitated for barely a millisecond, but once she answered him, her voice was strong and true. "I don't want to stop, not tonight, not with you. Take me, Cam. Make everything else go away. Make this night belong just to us."

Hell. That might just be an impossibly huge expectation to put on a lover…but a guy couldn't win what he didn't aspire to. So he tried. He concentrated five hundred percent of himself into every kiss, every caress. He tried tender, then rough. Tried an urgent, ardent rush, then the seductive frustration of slow hands and a lazy tongue.

Moonlight bathed her skin in silver. A nearby owl hooted, their only voyeur. And the scent of lavender kept seeping into his senses, into hers. When he finally swept her beneath him, his flesh seemed on fire, his muscles turgid and tight, drugged—crazy with her, for her.

She wrapped her long, slim legs around him even as he tested her soft center for moistness—as if she hadn't already told him in a thousand ways she was ready for him. Lips met and clung as he eased inside her, initially trying to be gentle, determined to be gentle. But she hissed his name in a fierce, frantic call, wooing him into her deeper, harder.

He plunged in then, burying his hands in her hair,

burying his lips in her lips, burying himself in the heart of her. It was crazy, totally crazy, but he had the sensation of belonging to her, belonging with her, in some emotional way he'd never even known existed before. This was about sex, he told himself. The best sex he'd ever had, but still, about sex.

The lie didn't last any longer than it took his mind to try it out. This was so *not* about sex it was shaking his world.

Or she was. She matched him, stroke for stroke, slamming heartbeat for slamming heartbeat, her lithe slick body tightening exactly when his did. She owned him at that moment. Or he owned her. Damned if he knew the difference—damned if he cared. The sky opened up in a shower of stars, or that's how he felt, as if he were flying over the moon with her, release pouring through him and into her.

For the briefest second he wished she hadn't answered his question about birth control, because this insane feeling of longing, belonging, owning was so compelling. He wanted his seed inside her, a child that came from the two of them. But that thought, like every other coherent thought, fled faster than moonbeams. They rode the crest together, then sank, both spent, in each other's arms.

Later…minutes later, hours later, Cameron opened his eyes. The moon was still up there, still framed in stars. The smells of earthy loam and lavender still pervaded his nostrils; somewhere a raccoon rustled and an owl hooted. He'd smelled the smells before, knew that moon. But he didn't know her; how it would feel to have her warm, vibrant body in his arms, still half-wrapped around him, her cheek nestled in the arch of his neck, her silky hair tickling his chin.

"Damn," he said.

She leaned back her head. "Uh-oh. That sounds like a man in the throes of regrets."

"Try again. I couldn't regret what just happened between us if my life were at stake." He bussed the top of her head, which made Charlie pop to attention again. He was too old to have Charlie pop to attention again this fast. It was her. Making him feel things, do things, want things that weren't *normal* for him.

He couldn't be in love with her. Not just because he barely knew the woman, but because his pull for her made no sense. She'd almost cried twice that day. Did he need a weepy woman? Did he need all those cats? For that matter, he'd seen Alps and ocean, so how could he possibly be drawn to some rocky land with red barns and stone fences and winding roads?

Perhaps more directly to the point, if he'd lost his mind, where the hell had it gone?

Was there a chance it could find its way home again?

"Cameron?" She twisted in his arms, not moving far away from him, just pushing back far enough that she could tilt her head and look at him face-to-face. Below, her fingers reached over and gently, playfully, entwined with his. ''Tell me about your daughters.''

He glanced down and watched their two hands blend together. Hell. Double hell. Teenagers held hands like this, not fully grown adults who were lying naked in the moonlight. But she didn't seem willing to sever all closeness yet, and neither was he.

The question about his daughters seemed to come from nowhere, but he was more than willing to answer it. Talk was better than the alternative—which was lying there, drinking in the scent of lavender and moonlight and wanting to make love to her again. So he talked. ''Miranda's fifteen. Kate's sixteen.'' He hesitated. ''For a long time it was totally clear cut that they belonged with their mom. It's not that I didn't want to be an active dad. I've always wanted that, always tried to be. I just traveled so much. Over the years, I always talked to them twice a week. We spend time together every holiday and school break. And I usually hang there at least a month every year to just be around them, part of their routine. Only lately…''

''Lately what?''

''Well, lately, they're fighting all the time with their mom. Most of it seems to be pretty standard teenage girl, mother stuff. Rules. Roles. But sometimes she's had it, and then I think…''

"You think what?"

"That if I lived in a more settled way, I could have them with me for a while. Most parents don't seem to like the teenage years, but for some strange reason, it doesn't bother me that they're being difficult and impossible. If anything, I feel like now I could be a better parent to them." Okay. He'd stripped naked some of his heart to tell her that. And left him hanging besides, so it was her turn now, he figured. "What about your ex?"

Her hand dropped away from his. She lay back, facing the stars. "Well…his name is Ed. Simpson, I always called him. Back in college, I took one look and just knew he was my first and only true love. He was a warm, family kind of guy, good sense of humor. Fun. I quit my last year of school to help him finish faster—he got his social work degree. He was always one to reach out to help someone else."

"Sounds like a saint," Cam said, and was briefly tempted to spit and paw the earth—but naturally he was too mature.

"Not exactly," she said wryly. "He's married to someone else now. In fact, they had their first child five months after the wedding. And he called me this morning to tell me about their newborn son."

"I don't understand why he'd call you." It wasn't hard for Cam to deduce that the creep had cheated on her, judging from the age of the first kid.

"Who would? I wouldn't take him back for a fortune, am over him in every way a woman can get over a man. For some reason he seems to still think I'm his friend. That we're still good friends.''

"So, are you?''

"No.''

"Then why on earth do you let him keep calling?''

"Because.'' She lifted a hand to the moonlight. "Oh, cripes, I don't know why. In the beginning, I acted friendly out of pride because I never wanted to let on how much he'd hurt me. And then I just didn't seem to know how to cut him off. I know they've really been struggling to afford their growing family.''

"Struggling? I thought your ex was wealthy.''

She frowned. "Why'd you think that?''

"Because…I thought you said or implied you'd gotten a pretty good settlement from the divorce. When you were talking about how you could afford to put up the greenhouses, not have to care if you lost money on the lavender, all that.''

"Oh. Well, I *did* get a good lump of money from the divorce—but not because Simpson gave me anything for free. We had a house together. He wanted to stay in the house to raise his kids, and I didn't need or want to stay there, so he owed me my share. Actually, I'd earned more than him back then. But the point was—''

It wasn't that hard to finish her sentence that time. "You wanted to spend any money you got from the marriage. It felt like ugly money somehow. As if it could sabotage your luck if you used it in a relationship with someone else.''

''Yeah. And I know that thinking was superstitious.''

''It is. But I remember feeling that way after my divorce, too. Then it wasn't about money. I gave her all the money I could, wanted her to have it. She had the girls. But the 'stuff'—furniture, paintings, the *things* we'd split up that were part of the marriage— at the time, it didn't matter how valuable they were or how much I liked them or even needed them. I wanted all ties severed.''

''So you understand. Why'd you get divorced, Cam?''

''I told you. Because I couldn't settle in one place. I was too restless. Not responsible enough. Not mature enough to make any kind of husband, either,'' he said honestly. ''And you?''

Her bare big toe had sneaked over and found his bare big toe. Now they were playing footsie, he realized. Both of them, like kids who couldn't stop touching each other. No matter what they were sure of and what they weren't.

There had to be something narcotic in the Vermont air. Something dangerous.

Maybe it was even in her big toe.

''Me, what?'' She seemed to be referring to some

question he'd asked, as if she'd lost track of the conversation.

Hell, so had he. "Why'd you get divorced? Because he cheated? Because you fell out of love? What?"

She didn't answer for a long time, and then finally she made a sound—like a wry little chuckle, only not so much humor in it. "We have a problem, Lachlan."

"What's that?"

"The problem is that I want to answer your question. I have this horrible feeling that you could turn out to be someone I could seriously trust. How weird is that?"

"Weird? You're not used to trusting people?"

She propped up on an elbow then. Moonlight draped the round of her shoulder, the edge of one plump, firm breast, the sweet soft curve of her hip and high. "Don't waste your time sounding surprised, Cam. You're no more used to trusting people than I am. You're a loner. Just like me."

He didn't know what to say, except that she didn't strike him as a natural loner in any conceivable way. She was an earth mother, a giving lover, a warm, nurturing woman right down to her toes. He said honestly, "I can well understand your needing time to get over a hurtful relationship, but in the long run it's impossible to imagine you living alone. Or not wanting to be in a marriage."

"I won't be climbing into another serious relationship," she said firmly.

He didn't believe her. But he said, "That's a relief, because I don't want to hurt you. And for darn sure, I won't lie to you. You know my work here's only temporary, that I'll be leaving soon. That's the way it has to be."

Again she smiled, at a moment when no other woman would have smiled at him. "And I'll be staying here. Because that's the way it has to be—for me. So we're both safe, right?"

"Safe?"

"Safe," she repeated. "You don't want to shake up my world. I don't want to shake up yours."

"Yes," he agreed.

"We do need to watch it, though," she said carefully. "I'm totally for casual sex. Especially with a man who's only going to be here for a short time, and who positively doesn't want anything serious from me. But we'll both get cranky if we start to seriously trust each other, so let's try not to, okay?"

She got up then. He didn't instantly understand that the conversation—and their lovemaking—was all done. In principle, they should have left an hour earlier at least. The night temperatures were dropping fast now, and the mosquitoes had come out to feast— still, he was shaking his head as he quickly gathered their gear together.

The woman he seemed to be falling for, very hard,

very fast, very irresponsibly, was walking toward his car completely naked in the moonlight. She didn't seem to find anything odd about that. She didn't seem to find anything odd about wanting to sleep with a man who wouldn't stick around for her, either.

But it bugged him.

It was never a good idea, to wake up the next morning without both people having agreed on what they needed from such an encounter. Only Violet's version of clearing the air had sure muddied his. Maybe most men would be happy to hear she was up for a short, passionate affair.

Maybe, even as early as last week, he'd have been ecstatic to hear a woman talk that way.

Only hearing Vi talk about casual sex and not wanting to trust him made him feel as edgy as if he'd sat on a porcupine. She deserved more than that. She should be demanding more from a man than that.

And damn it. He wanted to *be* more than that to her. Realizing how hard his heart was suddenly pounding, Cameron took a long, low, calming breath.

It had to be the moonlight. He just wasn't a man to think, or spell, a word as petrifying as commitment. Tomorrow—daylight—he'd get a grip on this whole thing. He just knew he would.

Eight

When Violet walked outside, the morning fog was magical. Pink dawn hues swirled in the mist. Drenched flowers and grass made the whole world sing with scent and color. It was her favorite kind of morning.

Today, though, she clumped toward her Herb Haven in mud boots and a scowl. She'd had hiccups twice already. Her stomach seemed to be doing a nonstop agitated jitterbug.

The Haven's parking lot already had four cars, even though it was barely seven. Customers were waiting for her. She gave an early class on Wednesday morning before the store opened, a class she normally loved to bits. But this morning her mind was entirely on the night before.

She'd never had casual sex before. It wasn't her fault. She'd always meant to fool around tons, but she'd fallen in love with Simpson young and there'd never been a chance. Now she was perfectly thrilled to throw her morals out the window, only it was all so awkward. She'd gone into her bedroom first last night, but she assumed Cameron would join her. Instead he'd gone into the spare room. And stayed there.

When you had mind-blowing fabulous sex with a lover, didn't you get to spend the night with him? What the hell were the rules to this deal, anyway? Cripes, it would resolve so many problems—and so much heartache—if she could just privately love someone and not have to worry about his caring about her long term.

Only, so far, this wasn't working at all. The sex part had been terrifyingly stunning. Only, she hadn't slept all night, first waiting for Cameron to come into her bed, and then worrying why he'd slept in the other room. And then there was that other tricky little problem.

She was crazy about the guy. More crazy than she could ever remember feeling before—even about Simpson. Cam was warm and funny and accepting and interesting and honest and everything she loved in a guy—not counting that naked-to-naked had been better than anything she'd ever dreamed of.

The *love* word had been on her mind even before they'd done the Deed. Making love had just made that worse.

She *knew* better than to let that *love* word enter the picture.

Glumly she opened the door to the Herb Haven. Lights were already on. Four women sat on the wooden table in the back, all talking at once and sipping her best coffee brew. They all knew where the key and coffeepot were; they knew the whole routine. Betsy and Harriet were farmers' wives; Roberta was a freshly divorced teacher; Dinah was a college student home for the summer with energy to burn. The women had nothing in common besides a history in White Hills—and wanting to make natural cosmetics at home.

"We're making cold cream today, right? Cold cream, aftershave and an herb bath." Violet heeled off her mud boots, plastered on a cheerful smile and charged in. Work would get her mind off Cam. It had to. "Did you ladies hear that Dora Ritter is pregnant? And everyone says it's Tom Johnson's, and his wife is pregnant at the same time."

"No!" Betsy said in delighted horror, and the women were off. Aprons were donned. Bowls and pots and measuring devices gathered from the cupboards, and then the core ingredients brought out.

Lanolin. Beeswax. Almond oil. Naturally Violet started making herb water first, and each of the women had chosen their favorite: lavender, rose, mint and lemon balm.

Smells pervaded the back room. Violet kept both the gossip and the work flowing, but no matter how fast she ran, her mind kept sneaking back to Cameron. She kept thinking, I want that man. I want to sleep with him. Love him. Laugh with him. And why shouldn't I? What's so wrong if two consenting adults both simply want to have a good time together?

"Violet, how long does this mess have to cook?" Betsy asked her.

Violet peered over the edge of the double boiler. "You're not trying to cook it. You just want the lanolin and beeswax to melt together. After that you add the almond oil."

"Gotcha."

"And at that point you call me, and I'll show you how we whisk in the herb water. You wanted the lemon balm, right?"

"Yeah, that was me. Harriet wanted the mint."

"Okay," she said, and thought: I can change. She didn't have to be a wife and mother. She could be an immoral, carefree lover who lived for today.

The more she thought about it, the more she realized how long she'd allowed the problem of her narrow fallopian tubes to get her down. So she'd been devastated to know she'd never likely conceive. So she'd been further crushed when Simpson had taken such a fast powder for another woman—a fertile woman—when Violet proved to be less than perfect.

I could do wicked, she figured. Obviously she'd have to work at it. She'd have to know the rules. She'd have to find someone she wanted to be wicked with—such as Cameron. In fact, specifically Cameron, since she'd never found anyone else she wanted to be wicked for…or with.

Turning into an amoral, immoral tramp would solve so many of her problems. Men were like perfume. Some had staying power. Some didn't. Counting on a guy to stick around just because he claimed to love you was the height of lunacy. It was far better to pick a guy from the get-go where you didn't have to feel bad about not being perfect.

"Hey, Violet. Come see how this is coming!"

Firmly, she turned her attention back to her class. Betsy, at the table's far end, was exuberantly slathering on her newly made almond cold cream. She'd come dressed today in a baseball cap, Jack Daniel's tee, and her favorite sequined tennis shoes. And then there was Harriet, who'd been married fifty-two years and could have starred in the infamous portrait of the two farmers carrying the pitchfork. Harriet had so many lines from the sun that the first three layers of cold cream seeped into the crevices and were never seen again. Roberta had been showing up for the classes ever since her divorce, wearing five pounds of mascara, a bra that pushed her boobs up to her throat, and fire-engine-red nail polish. And then there was Dinah.

"Hokay," Dinah drawled, "I think this aftershave lotion is finished. It was fun to make and all, but now I don't know what to do with it. Or how."

Harriet, ever wise, piped in, "Trust the one virgin in the group to make something for a man."

"Hey, who said I was a virgin?"

"The point, dear, is that we obviously need someone to test the aftershave on before you try giving it away as a present. Anyone have hairy legs? I mean, someone who's willing to admit it?"

Betsy, who always played Harriet's straight man, promptly burst out laughing. And because Betsy's laughter could make anyone laugh, within seconds the whole room was cracking up, holding stomachs and gasping guffaws and sputtering coffee—made worse as bare legs were lifted in the air as proof of their recent shaving—or lack thereof.

Silence fell as suddenly as a light switch. God knows how the rest of them realized there was a man in the room, but Violet sensed Cameron's sudden appearance from the instinctive change in her own heartbeat.

She whirled around to see him standing in the doorway, a steamy mug in one hand and a sheaf of papers in the other, looking wrinkled and sleepy and sexy. Wild. Wantable.

His eyes found hers as if there was no one else in the room. Last night suddenly danced between them—that surge of wanting, of urgency, of belonging, like she'd never felt for any man or anyone else. She'd never given herself that easily, that intimately.

And suddenly she wasn't so sure she could manage being as wicked and immoral as she wanted to be. Suddenly she sensed she could risk more with Cameron than she'd ever risked before—if she wasn't very, very careful.

The other women pounced on Cameron for entirely different reasons. "My God. He's the ideal test case," Dinah said.

Cameron tore his eyes off her and seemed to swiftly take in the others in the room. He may not have heard the gist of their earlier conversation, but he seemed to pick up fast that he was in trouble. He said, "No!" as if hoping that would cover everything.

"Now, there's nothing to worry about, dear. Come on. We just want to put a little bit of lotion on your cheek. It won't hurt. It's made of witch hazel and apple vinegar and lavender and sage—"

"Oh, my God. *No.*"

"It's supposed to make your skin feel really soft," Dinah assured him. "That's the whole point. To make it easier to shave—"

"Violet." His gaze swiveled back toward her. Desperately. "I just need to talk to you. About some business—"

Harriet said, "There now. Just sit down. You can do all the business you want with Violet and we can test our little aftershave recipe on you at the same time. You're not from Vermont, are you, but women here have been known to keep secrets for three and four centuries. No one will ever know you've been here, trust us. Don't be scared—"

He backed out of the doorway and took off like a bat out of hell.

She couldn't even try to catch up with him for several hours. She had to finish up the class and clean up, after which her two girls arrived to formally open the store for business. It was past ten before she could catch a five-minute stretch when the phone wasn't ringing or some customer asking for her.

Then, though, she had a hard time finding him. She looked in the house, in the yard, in the greenhouses. His car was still parked by the barns, so he hadn't left the property, but she was mystified where he might have walked. Finally she located him at her great-grandmother's cottage.

Decades ago the cottage had been built to give Gram independence in a way that would keep her close to family. No one had lived there after Gram died until Camille had come home in the spring. The place had been fixed up then—except for the roof.

That was the infamous roof she'd hired to have fixed so Cameron would have a place to stay. The roofer was supposed to show up this morning, but just like most mornings in a week, he'd neither showed nor called.

It was Cameron on top of the roof with a hammer in his hand, a box of shingles next to him. He'd yanked off his shirt, undoubtedly because of the sun beating down with baking intensity. His skin looked oiled and bronzed. All six cats were up there with him—either trying to help, or just wanting to be around the sexiest guy in three counties.

She felt the same way, but she stood below with her hands on her hips. "So. You've decided to take up a new career as a roofer?"

He turned around on a heel and rubbed a wrist on his damp forehead. "More likely a new career as escape artist. Those women aren't still around, are they?"

"No." Maybe last night was between them like an elephant in their emotional living room, but she still had to grin. "You're safe."

Apparently he wanted more proof. "And you don't have any of that smelly aftershave concoction anywhere around, do you?"

"Why, Lachlan. The girls *did* scare you. Imagine, a big strong guy like you—"

"I'm not *scared*," he said testily. "I just happened to come across this half-finished roof because of your cats. *They* were scared. Ran out of the place faster than I did and led me to the nearest high place.''

''You expect me to believe that half-baked story?''

''Look. I'm sure they were nice women. In fact, if I ever get attacked in the middle of the night by a gang of cutthroats, I'd really like them on my side. Especially the one—'' he motioned vaguely ''—you know. The one who'd rearranged the shape of her—''

''Breasts.''

''Yeah. So that they looked like two oranges poking out right under her chin. And the one with the hairy legs—you know, the one who looked as if she had more wrinkles than a Shar Pei? Look, it's just a lot safer up here—''

''You're killing me.'' Damn man. They'd gotten into serious, deep waters last night. Mighty deep waters. Yet somehow he was making her comfortable, making her laugh.

He squinted down at her, his voice quieting. ''Well, chère, it damn near killed me to sleep down the hall from you last night.''

Her pulse suddenly seemed to careen down a long, sleek hill. Who'd have guessed he would confront her hurt, confused feelings straight up? She took a breath. ''Then why did you?''

''Because of the lavender. Because until we get some legal details discussed and agreed on, I'm representing Jeunnesse. That doesn't have to be a complication. But I don't want you worrying for even a minute that it could be." He lifted a sheaf of papers from his side. "Have you got fifteen minutes to look at these?"

"Cam, I *hate* legal mumbo-jumbo," she groused, but her pulse careened back up that long, sleek hill. So he hadn't slept in the other room because he hadn't wanted to be with her. And he was sure as hell still looking at her as if she were sugar and he was more than happy to take on the role of hummingbird.

"It won't hurt, I promise. And no one will find us out here, so without interruptions, we can get it done fast."

"I really don't have a bunch of time. I can't leave the girls alone for very long. They're both really young—"

He heard all her protests, but he still had them sitting together on the porch steps of the cottage and the papers whipped out faster than lightning. He might be determined to talk, but Violet couldn't seem to concentrate on his silly papers. His knee was grazing hers. She wasn't sure if the touch was accidental, or if he was deliberately keeping in physical contact. But knees had never struck her as an intimate, erogenous zone before. Still didn't. His knee was bony, his legs long and lanky and tanned, leading to sandals. Long feet. Very long. Really long big toes.

"…patent?" he asked.

"Hmm?"

"Patent, Violet. We're talking about your applying for a patent for the new breeds of lavender you developed."

"Okay."

He sighed. "One of us doesn't seem to be concentrating, because 'Okay' doesn't answer the question. The question is—did you apply for a patent?"

"Um, no, not exactly."

"In other words, no. All right. But listen seriously for a minute, okay? Because you need to know this. You want to patent both the product and the process. They're two separate things. So I'm going to apply for both those patents in your name. It takes forever before you actually get your patents, but just by applying and starting the process, you have some serious legal protections."

As boring and tedious as all this junk sounded, she started to feel guilty. "Cam, you don't have to do this. I'll get around to it, honestly."

"No, you won't. You've started yawning every time we started talking about this, and I can see the same suffering expression on your face now. So I'll get the applications started. But if anyone else tries this on you, you say no, hear me? Because you can't just go around trusting people."

"Did you think I was worried you were going to cheat me?"

"You should be worried," he said sternly.

"Gotcha." She tried to look more attentive, but he was so right about the subject being boring—and he wasn't. Besides which, his protectiveness was adorable, even if he did have knobby knees and really, really long big toes. His eyelashes were blond. Long and wonderful, but unless you were close enough to notice—which she was—you'd never realize they were so long and thick. And God, those eyes.

"You have to have a name for the strain of lavender you created. I don't suppose you might have one in mind?"

"Sure do!" At last, a question she had answer for. "Moonlight."

He paused. "*That's* the name you want? Moonlight lavender?"

"Yup. My lavender isn't as dark a purple as some strains, but it has a color that seems almost... translucent. A rich purple, almost as if the color seems lit from within. The way the light shines from the moon, you know?"

He looked as if he wanted to comment—possibly Moonlight wasn't too formal a botanical name? But whatever, he changed his mind about commenting, plugged a pencil behind his ear and went on.

And on.

And on.

Sheesh, all this serious stuff and information kept

pouring from his mouth. How Jeunnesse wanted to handle the lavender. What she could choose or not choose to be involved in. Exactly what he needed to put in motion over the next three weeks; what would happen after the harvest. What she would get for this, for that, for the next thing. How she was protected. What her choices were, but also how she shouldn't listen to him. The type of attorney and accountant she should call to help her understand the ramifications of her choices.

"All right," Cam said finally. "Now there's just one more thing before I can get this started."

"Shoot," she said, thinking that she just might curl up in his lap and snooze if they had to talk this kind of business much longer.

"Maybe you think I should take this answer for granted—but I can't. You *do* know what you did, right? You *can* reproduce it?"

"You mean, can I reproduce the strain of lavender I developed out there?" When he nodded in agreement, she lifted a hand. "Beats me. I don't know."

"Vi."

"What?"

"Quit with the blonde talk. I was only fooled the first day. You know more about this than a chemist any day of the week. In fact, you could probably teach classes at Harvard. So quit goofing off and tell me straight. Can you reproduce how you did this or not?"

"I'll have you know I'm as flaky as they come," she defended herself.

"You can do flaky," he agreed, obviously not wanting to insult her. "In fact, you could win an Oscar for how well you do flaky. But right now you're just talking to me. I'm not going to tell anyone you're brilliant if you want it kept a secret. But before we go any further with the patent process, or the harvest, I need to know. Could you go into another greenhouse and reproduce these strains? Or would we only be cloning the plants you have on the twenty acres out there?"

She was starting to feel miffed. Every guy in the neighborhood thought she was a ditsy blonde. It had been easy to fool them. Easy to fool the whole world—or at least the male half of it. So why did Cam have to be so damned different? "I'll answer the question only if you'll answer one for me."

"So go."

"All right. Then yes, I can recreate this nature of lavender anywhere. It took working with about four different strains and some specific growing techniques and conditions, but it wasn't a fluke. I planned the experiments. I knew what I was doing." She said firmly, "So now it's your turn to answer a question."

"Let's hear it."

"Is that really the reason you took off for the spare room last night? Because of some idiotic ethics thing?"

"Idiotic… What can I say? I'm sorry. I take ethics really seriously. It's a character flaw I've never completely been able to shake."

If he teased her anymore, she might just have to slap him. Instead, she asked him the crux of the question. "So. We did the ethics thing. Now what. Are we going to sleep together while you're here or not?"

"We are. We definitely are," he said, as if the question hadn't surprised him in the slightest. His tone was low, fervent and very, very clear. So was the way he looked at her. "And damn soon."

Nine

"Good afternoon, ladies." Cameron walked into the kitchen. At least he was wearing a T-shirt this time, but after spending two solid weeks in the sun, his bronzed skin in shorts and sandals still made five pairs of eyes instantly swivel in his direction.

"Hi, Cameron!"

"Hi, Cameron, how's it going?"

"Good to see you, again, Cam!"

Violet rolled her eyes. Two weeks ago, Cameron would have broken out in an alpha-male sweat to see four women, sitting in bathrobes at the kitchen table, slathered in white-purple face masks and sipping wine. Now, he cheerfully fielded their greetings, reached in the refrigerator for a cold soda and promptly hiked back outside.

The tableful of women let out a collective sigh. Once a month, Violet put on a ''pamperfest,'' not because she needed more to do, but because the products she used invariably brought more customers. Today's agenda had included a facial mask made from oatmeal and lavender, a foot soak and a conditioner for damaged hair. The conditioner was her own private recipe of geranium, lavender, sandalwood and rosewood, all diluted in vegetable oil, rubbed in the hair and covered in a towel for two hours.

At this point in the proceedings, all four women had the face masks on and the conditioner slathered in their hair. Originally she'd served a cooled herbal tea, but Maud Thrumble—typically—had slipped two bottles of wine onto the table before they'd even started.

''God, he's such a hulk,'' Maud said fervently.

''Hunk, not hulk,'' Mary Bell corrected her. ''Quit trying to be cool when you don't know the terms. You're so old you'd probably have called him a dreamboat in your day.''

''Whatever,'' Maud said. She and Mary Bell had never gotten along all that well. ''He's to die for. That's the point. If only I hadn't been married for fifty years, I'll tell you, I'd give him a good run for his money.''

The other two women hooted at this news, causing

a bowl of lavender-oatmeal goo to spill and Violet to leap up for a rag.

"Aw, Violet, leave it be. We'll all clean it up when we're through."

"It's all right," she said.

"No, it's not." Sally Williams frowned at her. "You've been quiet all afternoon, not like yourself. What's wrong?"

"Not a thing. In fact, everything's hunky-dory. Smooth as silk. Georgy-peachy. Totally copacetic." In fact, if things got any better, she'd have to smash her head into a door. Edgy as a wet cat, Violet swiped at the spill on the floor, then aimed for the sink. If a woman was going to make a mess, it was her theory that a woman should make a good one. Her entire kitchen looked like a witch's trash. Clay and porcelain pots of herbs spilled over the counters. Leaves and stems and flowers strewed from the door to the sink. And the pot that mixed the oatmeal and lavender—God knew how she was going to clean it. "What's not to be happy? It's a gorgeous day. Life's good—"

"Enough, already," Maud said. "It's that man that's gotten you down, isn't it?"

"What man?" She'd never been less depressed, Violet told herself. The last couple weeks had been wonderful. Every day had been sunny. Her Herb Haven business was busier than a swarm of bees. Cameron had taken over the lavender harvest completely, hiring Filbert Green, the local farmer who'd taken care of the land after the parents retired. At this very moment, in fact, there was a crew in the lavender, unseen, unheard, none of whom had bothered her for anything.

Family news had been just as peaceful. Camille had called to wax poetically on the wonders of honeymoons with teenagers. Her mom had called to convey that she and her dad had been going to vacation in Maine and somehow taken a wrong turn; they were headed for New Zealand. And Daisy hadn't called—which was yet another good thing—because when she connected with her oldest sister the next time, Violet planned to strangle her. Daisy was very good at getting her sisters embroiled with men, but when it came to revealing what she was doing herself, suddenly she took a powder, probably somewhere on the Riviera on a nude beach.

Violet opened the fridge, put the dish rag on the top shelf and closed it. When she turned around, the women were all staring at her.

"What? What?"

"Vi, you're just not yourself today," Sally repeated. "Sit down and have some wine, girl."

"It's four in the afternoon. If I have wine now, I'll be curled up on the floor before dinner."

"Well, something stronger then. How about a little strawberry daiquiri?" From nowhere, Mary Bell lifted a delicate sterling silver flask in the air. Sally promptly zoomed for the cupboard and brought down a glass, then cleared a seat of damp towels so Violet could sit down. "Speaking of alcohol—"

"I didn't think we were."

That was ignored. "It looks as if your houseguest is doing something illegal out there. At least in my daddy's day, we used to call that kind of device a still. He making moonshine on you?"

"No. He's making lavender oil...or 'lavender absolute' as it's properly called, I guess. It's kind of hard to explain the process." She stared at the glass of cherry daiquiri in front of her, then thought what the hell and took a sip. "First you have to pick the flowers when only two thirds of the florets are opened up. Then...well, come to think of it, the distilling process probably does have something in common with a bootlegger's still. You put water in one container and the flowers in another. You heat the water hot enough to make steam, and then that's pushed through a pipe under high pressure through the plant material. The steam works to separate or displace the water from the oil. The oil always..."

"Good grief," Maud said. "You're going to make our eyes cross. None of us give a holy damn about the still business, dear, we were just trying to get you talking. You haven't had a man near you since you came home after the divorce, and suddenly you've got this gorgeous hulk living with you—"

"Hunk," Mary Bell corrected.

"Whatever. The point is that your mother isn't here, but we all know she'd be hoping that you're taking advantage of the situation."

Violet gulped down another sip of daiquiri, feeling cornered. Furthermore, her cats had all hunkered on top of the refrigerator, away from the bawdy, noisy drinkers with their increasingly stiff facial masks. "He's not *living* with me. He's just living here. Until the roof for the cottage is done—which was supposed to have been finished a whole month ago. In fact, almost two months ago now. I can't make Bartholomew show up regularly for work to save my life."

"That's roofers, dear. I should know. I was married to one for twelve years. He only showed up on time for dinner twice, God rest his soul." Anne Blayton almost never spoke up, but she'd finished two glasses of wine now. Her mask was starting to crack like old parchment. "He sure was good between the sheets, though."

"Well, you've been through enough husbands, you should be a judge," Mary Bell said sweetly.

"The point," Maud said, "is not whether he's sleeping here or in the cottage, but where he's not sleeping when the lights go out. Are you deaf and blind, Violet Campbell? Last week, with that ghastly heat wave, I swear the only redeeming part of my day was to drive past here and see him walking in the yard, at least half the time without a shirt. Whooee."

"I hadn't noticed." Violet reached forward to pour a little wine into her now-empty glass.

"Violet, honey, you just added wine to your daiquiri," Mary Bell said kindly. "You're just not yourself."

"I am *too* myself."

The back door opened again. Cameron ambled in. "Hi, ladies. Looks like you're having fun." He deposited an empty can in the trash, smiled at the group, stroked three cats and ambled through to the other room.

Four women let out another collective sigh. All of them were smiling hard enough to crack their masks. "It's time we washed you all off," Violet said firmly.

That was at least three times he'd walked in this afternoon. Three times, when he'd laughed and joked with the women. It wasn't that long ago that he would have had a cow and a half over an estrogen-loaded event like this. He didn't run anymore. He didn't act terrified—or even surprised—if he wandered into the kitchen and found a roomful of masked women with their bare feet in buckets, sitting in bathrobes in the middle of the afternoon.

It just wasn't natural. He was beyond being the ideal guy—helping her with everything from dishes to chores, making the whole lavender thing look effortless, doing his own wash, never taking over the remote, bringing groceries in. He'd quit trying to finish the roof, but that was only because he'd completely run out of spare time. Normal men only helped out if they were harassed, blackmailed or wanted sex. Everybody knew that. Cameron seemed to think it was ordinary behavior to pitch in. More confusing yet, he took every damn thing in her life in stride, as if it were all very interesting, instead of the nature of stuff that should have given an alpha guy like him nightmares.

Instead, he'd been giving *her* nightmares.

As soon as the women were cleaned up and herded out, Violet piled dishes into the sink, added sudsy water and then turned on the dishwasher. A moment later she realized she'd turned the dishwasher on without any dishes in it, and thought she'd either had too much to drink…

Or too little Cameron.

She looked frantically around for the dish towel, but it seemed to have disappeared.

Two weeks ago he'd claimed he wanted to sleep with her. Intended to sleep with her. Imminently soon.

Only, they hadn't.

He'd been kissing her regularly. Over breakfast. Before lunch. In the middle of the day, if he found her in the Herb Haven with her hands filled with a dried-herb arrangement, he'd take a bite out of the back of her neck, cup her fanny. He'd walked with her in the moonlight. They'd hip-danced doing the dishes after dinner, barged in on each other coming out of the bathroom, fallen asleep watching horror movies on the same couch.

But the damn man hadn't done one thing about seriously seducing her. She was free! She was cheap! She was available. She had boobs. She wasn't asking him for a single thing! So what was the matter with the man?

Upstairs, she heard the pipes rattle. He was taking a shower. She opened the refrigerator for some God-unknown reason and found her dish towel. She held the cool towel to her pounding head. The man was turning her into a train wreck. She had to get her life back. She couldn't remember where her shoes were, her keys, her dishrags. She was starting to become ditsy for real.

Enough was enough. If Mohammed wasn't willing to come to the mountain, she was darn well going to have to try seducing the mountain herself.

Cameron walked into the kitchen and stopped dead. They'd been sharing KP duty over the past couple weeks, but after seeing the war zone caused by the women's group earlier, he'd put on clean khakis and a decent shirt, figuring that Violet would want to go out to dinner.

Instead, the women were gone and the kitchen cleaned to within an inch of its life—give or take the cats and cat hair. The old oak table had white quilted place mats, roses floating in a bowl, some kind of wild salad—smelled like lemon-pepper shrimp—puffed-up fresh rolls…

Violet whirled around. ''We're having something I call come-to-Bahama wings. They're chicken wings without the bones. Kind of hot. A little lime juice, some rum, some honey, some hot peppers… I guess I should have asked you first, but you can handle hot, can't you, Lachlan?''

''Sure,'' he said, but the adrenaline was instantly pumping. Something was wrong. Worrisome wrong. The way she smiled at him raised the temperature in the kitchen twenty degrees. He saw the hot wings and the roses and heard the come-to-mama invitation in her voice.

Everywhere he looked, there were more land mines. And the more he looked, the more he recognized that she'd gone to a ton of trouble, laying all kinds of intricate, tricky traps.

She was barefoot, wearing a skirt that looked like a long, floaty handkerchief. Her midriff was bare, her long hair all scooped up and twisted and sedated with long clips off her neck. Said neck had been doused with some lethal scent—not her usual citrus soap, for damn sure, but something that reached his nostrils from the doorway. The perfume was a drug. That was all he was sure of.

Her lips had been coated with something shiny, and she was wearing a top that looked like another handkerchief. Only the top was actually about the size of a handkerchief this time, such a light fabric that he could clearly make out the plump swell of her breasts and the shape of her nipples.

"Whew, it's really hot tonight, isn't it?" she said with a grin.

His bloodstream shot his heart another dose of adrenaline. Yeah, he'd suspected that patience—and celibacy—would pay off eventually. But Violet was usually so warm and nurturing that he'd never figured she'd be the kind of woman to play mean.

This setup wasn't just mean; it was down and dirty.

"I figured you had such a swamped afternoon that you'd want to go out, pick up dinner. Hell, I'd have helped if I'd known you were going to all this trouble."

"No trouble," she said sweetly. "You've been working crazy long hours yourself. I decided that we both needed some real food and a relaxing evening for a change."

"Relaxing," he echoed, thinking that nothing about this setup was remotely relaxing. On the other hand, even in ninety-degree heat after putting out a ten-hour work day, his entire body was hard as stone. Hard, willing and high on anticipation.

However, he hadn't sucked it up and slept alone the past two weeks just to let her get off this easy. Yeah, he was willing to kiss her feet—and all the way up from there. But he hadn't deprived himself, or her, without reason. He smiled at her as if his blood wasn't pounding, ambled up behind her and dropped a soft, slow kiss on the drift of her nape. "What can I do to help?"

He felt her responsive shiver—but she recovered too darn fast. "Nothing but enjoy the feast. Or...how about if you pour the wine? It's red. I know you're supposed to have white wine with fish and chicken, but I didn't have any around...and red is so much more potent, don't you think?"

Another glossy, sultry smile, another tip of the lashes. He thought, I'll be lucky to make it through dinner without throwing her on the table and going for it. "Yeah, I like red better than white, too. Hey..."

"Yes?"

Somehow he had to buy some time. He was more than willing to let her have her way. But first he wanted to understand what had motivated all these sudden wicked tactics of hers—not that he wasn't enjoying them. Just that he figured a few minutes of distracting conversation was a good idea. "I was thinking how crazy it was that we've been together every day, yet I never asked you what you did. I mean, I know you moved here after a divorce and set up your herb business. But what kind of work did you do before that?"

"Work?" The question obviously startled her, because momentarily she forgot the sultry-smile, big-eye thing.

"Yeah. I mean, for a living. Were you into some kind of different career before this?"

There went the last of the provocative smile and the hip sashaying. It wasn't as if she didn't still look sexy as hell, and then some, but as if she stopped planning it.

She handed him dishes, one after the other, and he carted them to the table. Within minutes they were eating. A half hour later they were on the last bites and their second glass of wine.

"I was a physical therapist," she told him. "I didn't have any kind of formal specialty or anything fancy like that. But I mostly worked with kids. Kids who'd been in accidents, lost a limb or use of a limb. Tough road, to get a little one physically and emotionally prepared for life again, after going through a trauma to that extent."

Cameron shook his head, no longer stalling or playing games. He was fascinated by everything she'd been telling him. "Wow. I can't believe you never mentioned this before."

"There was no reason to. I'm not doing it now."

He hesitated. He could see in her face there was more here. He sensed Violet kept the "more" to herself for reasons he couldn't fathom. So he pressed. "You quit because you burned out on it?"

"No. Not exactly. Kids tend to hate physical therapy. Actually, adults do, too. It's not fun. It hurts and it's hard work. And especially for children who've been through a life-changing event, they feel confused and angry about what's happened to them. Anger, fear, frustration. I can't explain this, but that's exactly why I loved the work—at the time. Have some more wings, Cam."

"I couldn't eat another bite. So you really liked working with children, huh?"

She snapped her fingers and jumped up. "I'll bet I can coax you into eating one more thing. How about a little dish of vanilla-bean ice cream? With a little drizzle of raspberry rum sauce over it?"

"Whatever you can handle, I can handle," he said.

She shot him a look. By then the sun was skating down the horizon, turning the treetops a velvet green and the sky a silky azure. One cat opened her eye at the word *ice cream* but otherwise the herd was snoozing at a distance, too lazy to even beg.

"Well then, hon, I'll just dish you up a big dollop of trouble," Vi promised him.

As if she hadn't done that from the second he met her. Right then, though, Cameron wasn't willing to be completely diverted from the bone he was determined to pick. "So…why aren't you still doing the physical therapist thing?"

He saw a sudden flash in her eyes, the slightest stiffening in her shoulders. "Because when I came home, I started the Herb Haven."

Which didn't answer his question in the slightest. "And that's obviously gone great for you," he said smoothly, "but you weren't inclined to find work as a physical therapist in White Hills? Or weren't there any PT jobs here?"

"No. There's probably work. There's a good-size clinic in White Hills. I just—"

"You just what?" He smiled at her as he poured her another glass of wine.

"I just decided that maybe I should stop working with children for a while. Do something else. Everyone doesn't stay in the same job forever."

"No, they don't. In fact, I never got it, why people felt obligated to find one career and stick to it. What's so wrong about liking change? Wanting to do new things, see new horizons?"

"Exactly. People don't have just one dream," she said defensively.

"They sure don't." Yet he was almost sure that Vi still did have that one dream about working with kids. Not because he had extrasensory perception. But because there seemed a haunted unhappiness in her eyes, a tension.

"Change is fun," she agreed. "What's not to love about new challenges? Doesn't everybody need to stretch their minds? Not fall into a rut?"

"That's really true...but, damn, I have the hardest time imagining you falling into any kind of rut. You bring a sense of fun and adventure into everything you do. Other people get bored. You seem to find a spirit of fun in everything.''

She glowed for a second, then jumped up on him again, all flustered. ''All right. That's enough being nice to me. About time we talked about you. In fact, I've been wondering—''

''No,'' he said mildly, not responding to her words but to her actions. He suspected that she was about to make a deliberately catastrophic amount of noise, banging around the kitchen—an effective way to cut off any further serious conversation. ''Let's leave the dishes for now. How about if we take the ice cream out on the porch swing and see if we can scout up a breeze?''

Typically, she was willing to do anything to get out of dishes so she agreed. She bought out the ice-cream dishes, not little dishes, like she'd claimed, but major masterpieces with her fancy sauce. The smell of rum was wildly sweet and strong, adding to the other nectar smells of the evening. He exclaimed over the dessert. She laughed. Yet it was Violet who spooned one bite and then put her dish on the ground.

Before he could ask another personal question— and, for damn sure, before he could get her to talk about her work with children again—she suddenly stole his dish, too. Set it on the ground in the sun, next to hers. And plopped in his lap.

A guy always hoped to win the lottery, but he didn't expect it. Her fanny nestled in his lap, as if seeking the exact weight and pressure that would drive him crazy. She found it easily. Before he could even breathe, her arms had swooped around his neck. For all that sudden impulsiveness, though, she leaned closer and only offered him a whisper of a kiss. The graze of her mouth against his was soft, light, silky.

"Hey," he whispered. "What's happening here?"

"You don't want me to kiss you?"

"Oh, yeah, I do." And all his control buttons snapped. The power outage of '03 had nothing on this moment. He'd waited and waited and waited to taste her again, and here she was, warm and willing and almost bare, obviously intent on inviting him to take what he'd been craving for the past two weeks.

So he let her test him with that teasing little kiss of hers and then came back, pirate fast, with another kind of kiss entirely. He didn't want her lips; he wanted her whole mouth, her tongue. He didn't want a sweet sample; he wanted saliva and combustible heat. He wanted her heart pounding. He wanted her eyes to open wide with awareness and worry—not *bad* worry, but he was definitely tired to hell of her thinking she was safe around him. He wanted her to know that she wasn't safe. And neither was he.

He got everything he wanted and then some. When her lashes shuttered open, she looked dazed and more than a little shook up. "Well," she said faintly, on the gust of a pale breath. "I guess you *did* want to kiss me."

But he couldn't come up with any more easy smiles. "You really thought I didn't?"

"You didn't seem to have any problem walking into your own room all these nights. You didn't even try to—"

"Seduce you?"

"I don't need to be *seduced,* Lachlan. I'm a grown woman. But I just didn't understand what the deal was."

"Neither did I, chère." He pushed back a strand of hair that had sneaked free from all those clips holding it back. "I knew I wanted you. I knew you were willing to make love with me. But I kept having the bad, bad feeling that you were going to regret it."

That startled her. "Why did you think I'd regret sleeping with you? I never said—"

"I know you 'never said' anything specific. But you only said you were willing to make love when you pegged me as the kind of man who wouldn't give a damn about you, wouldn't stick around." When she tried squirming and doing her flutter-the-hands thing, he gently cuffed her wrist. "The fact is, I do care. I do give a damn. And nothing I understand about you, sensed about you, made me believe you were being truthful. If you want a short fling, trust me, Vi, I'd be happy to give you one. But I can't buy it. That you're going to be okay to just hit the sheets and then go our different ways the next morning. Or the next week.''

She took a hard breath. Then pushed off his lap and stood. So did he. As if the porch had suddenly become unbearably claustrophobic, she suddenly vaulted down the porch steps and started walking. So did he. Restless or not, it was still tepid hot, still too humid to breathe. She didn't run any farther than the deep shade of the maple, and then she turned on him.

''You want to know the deal, Lachlan? It's that I have skinny tubes. That's the deal. The whole deal. The chance of my ever having kids is mighty unlikely.''

Aw, hell. The minute she blurted that out, Cameron wanted to slug himself. God knew how he'd missed it, because immediately he realized she'd given him a ton of clues. Her reproducing plants so wildly. Her endless herd of cats. Her not going back to a profession with children. The way she mothered the two girls who worked for her. He even remembered—now, too damn late—the funny look on her face when she'd first said she didn't need birth control. ''That's about as unfair as it gets, chère,'' he said softly.

''More than unfair. I never wanted fancy things. Forget the riches and jewels and all that. I just wanted a house and kids and a man to love.'' Her head shot up, her eyes jewel bright. ''And you're wondering what that has to do with our making love.''

"No. I wasn't wondering anything. I was just feeling bad for you."

"Yeah, well. The thing is…maybe there was a time I wouldn't have been comfortable with casual sex. But that was then. And this is now. I've been alone since the divorce. That's three years."

"Hey," he said gently. Hell's bells, those tears were welling up. And yeah, of course he knew she cried at the drop of a hat. Only, damn it, this time she had reason to cry, a terrible huge reason to cry, and that was way different from seeing her cry at a Kodak commercial. He scooped her close, stroking her back, feeling her shudder back a real sob, afraid that she was going to do it seriously to him this time—cry until they were both drenched.

"I don't want a husband," she said fiercely.

"You don't have to have a husband."

"I've been trying to scare men away for three years. And doing a *great* job of it."

"You're great at being ditsy," he reassured her, and stroked, stroked, stroked. "But maybe you don't have to work at it quite so hard. It's not like every man wants kids—"

"I *know* that. But I also had a husband who took off the minute he found out I was…flawed. Yes, he wanted kids. And so did I. But we could have made other choices—like adopting or fostering. That's when I realized it wasn't as simple as just being about kids. It was about his seeing me differently, seeing me as less of a woman. My feeling like less of a woman.''

He stopped stroking. ''Wait a minute. What kind of horse hockey is this?''

''It's not horse hockey, Lachlan. You asked me what the deal is, and I'm telling you. In the beginning I just didn't see a reason to get into all this. It wasn't your problem, wasn't your business. But you asked so I'm telling you. I want to get into casual sex. With you. I want to know for sure that you're leaving. That you're going back to your own life. That I don't have to worry about how you think about me as a woman, deep down. How you—''

Damned if he was going to let her finish another idiotic sentence. Enough was enough.

Ten

Violet felt completely bewildered when Cameron suddenly grabbed her. She'd been trying to seriously talk to him. She was all riled up and upset that the whole crappy story about her skinny tubes had come out. She'd never wanted Cam to know. It was fine the way it was. Good the way it was. He thought of her as a whole, sexy woman—she knew he did. She didn't want him to see her differently, and she'd been afraid all along that he would if he knew the whole blasted picture.

Yet suddenly his arms swept around her, tighter than a noose, and his mouth swooped down on hers, slapped hers, crushed hers…then almost immediately lightened. Slower than honey, a taking kind of kiss became a wooing kind of kiss. A coaxing, wooing kind of kiss suddenly became an ardent, Iwantyou needyou havetohaveyou kind of kiss. His tongue found hers. His hands sieved into her hair. She felt his long, hard body throb against hers, and suddenly she was trembling from the inside out.

He was going to take her. She knew it in the flash of an instinct, a burst of heat and fear and excitement streaking through her pulse. Right here, right now, right under the deep, dark shade of the maple. No one was around, and the sun was setting fast now, but heaven knew strangers and neighbors both drove by and drove in at all hours.

It was as if he didn't care. Didn't notice.

And then neither did she.

She'd never felt like this. As a young girl, she'd dreamed incessantly all that tedious stuff about the prince who'd find her, who'd make her the center of his world, who'd slay dragons for her. But obviously she'd grown up. There were no fairy tales, and she'd wanted a flesh-and-blood guy and not a fake prince anyway. But Cameron…oh, Cameron.

He pushed at clothes, buttons, zippers. Heeled off his shoes, lifted her out of hers. No one had ever swept her away like this. Made her feel as if he couldn't breathe without her breath, couldn't survive without touching her, couldn't live. Without having her.

His eyes were open on hers, intense, unrelenting. Yet his mouth kept coming, even as he swooped her down to the ground on their makeshift nest of clothes. A car went by, maybe saw them, maybe didn't.

Pagan kiss followed pagan kiss, each more fierce and wild than the last. A button dug into her spine. Grass tickled. Her hair tangled—her darn long hair was always tangling—yet only one thing mattered to her. Cam. And what they seemed to be creating together.

When he suddenly lifted his head, she tried to say something, but the way he looked at her dammed all the words in her throat and her heart was suddenly hammering, hammering. "I *love* you," he said roughly. "*Love,* Vi. Do you hear me?"

Again she tried to answer, but he moved so fast. One instant he was taking her mouth, the next he'd twisted around, all naked and bronzed and bare, and started over completely at the other end. He kissed her right foot, from arch to toe, then worked his way up. Kisses wreathed from ankle to knee to the inside of her thigh to the core of her, and when she was gasping for breath, he flipped her over. He kissed her fanny; bit softly, tenderly, then laved a silken path up her spine to the nape of her neck. Then flipped her again.

His tongue dove into her mouth, mated with hers, even as he reached down. He wrapped her legs around his waist, intimately tight, and then dove in, drove in, taking her high and tight and intimately. Desire suddenly developed sharp teeth. Need clawed at her, ached through her. The need for completion, but even more, the need to love. Him. To be loved. By him.

"Come with me," he rasped. The sun dropped so fast, as if understanding they needed privacy, yet the darkness so stealthily brought voyeurs. Crickets. Frogs. Lightning bugs. Cats. And then the moon.

Their moon.

She saw his face above her, so sharply honed, so full of passion and emotion, even as she could feel herself losing any last ounce of control. Love reeled through her, whipped through her senses and heart.

"*Now*, Vi," he said.

She came with him, feeling as if she were free-falling from the top of the sky. But not alone. She fell with Cam, wildly, from the heart. Even minutes later, even hours later, she couldn't shake the flushed, joyous sensation of feeling totally complete. Totally whole. As if she were the most powerful woman ever born, woman with a capital *W*, the woman she'd always wanted to be.

Cam's woman.

And at that moment she couldn't imagine feeling any other way.

Cameron couldn't sleep.

It had to be well past two in the morning. They'd

eventually made it to her bedroom, dozed for a while, wakened to make love all over again. Now, oddly, he was more wide awake than a hoot owl. She was lying in his arms, damp, warm, draped all over him— or he was draped all over her. Who cared who was doing the draping as long as every inch of his skin was touching every inch of hers?

His eyes were used to the darkness now. He kept staring at the silver moonlight flooding in the open window, the quiet stir of curtains, the pale light falling on that strangely austere bedroom. "Vi," he whispered.

"Hmm?"

He'd been pretty sure she was awake, just not positive. Her voice was sleepy, sated, content—but awake. "*Chère,* are you absolutely positive about the infertility?"

She didn't stiffen in his arms this time, which told Cameron that she was okay talking about the subject with him now. The trust was there. For him. For her. "Let's put it this way," she said with a wry touch of humor. "Originally I learned everything about sex from Simpson—which means that I learned almost everything wrong. From the time we were in high school, Simpson made me think that a guy had to get off or he suffered terribly. That guys couldn't wait. That sometimes girls made it and sometimes they didn't, but overall, that Real Women did."

"As in...it's the woman's fault if she doesn't have a climax?"

"Yup. I can't believe I swallowed a lot of the things Simpson used to tell me. And on the baby subject, he really believed that it must be the woman's fault if she couldn't get pregnant, if the guy was virile." She sighed. "Some things he didn't have completely wrong. He had his sperm checked. And they were all aggressive little swimmers. I was the one with the skinny tubes." She snuggled closer. "You know what?"

"What?"

"I didn't want to tell you about all this, but... somehow it's opened my eyes to just air it all out. It's obvious to me now what I was doing with the lavender. I needed to create something that was totally my own, something that came specifically from me. And I guess I did go a little batty with enthusiasm."

"A little?"

He heard her soft chuckle in the darkness. "Okay. So I went hog wild. But the thing is—I never thought all my experiments would take. I thought most of them would miscarry, you know? Why should they work? I was a novice at this, no more than a closet gardener. It just seemed to be luck, that everything I touched reproduced with no problem. It was so ironic."

"Ironic in what way?" He stroked that long hair,

knowing she'd be annoyed in the morning she hadn't braided it, but loving it loose.

"Ironic, because all I had to do was love it. And nurture it. And it thrived." She sighed. "Same with cats. I took in one stray barn cat three years ago. He was starved, crippled. I didn't think he had a chance of making it, and the next thing I knew, he'd miraculously turned into a she-cat and had kittens on me." She stroked his neck, as if somehow instinctively knowing where he liked being touched most. "My mom had this theory, raising kids."

"Which was?"

"Which was that everybody's powerful in some way. We just have to clue in to who we naturally are. My mom taught us girls that each of us had something in our nature that we needed to listen to, develop. For me, I thought it was to be a mother. To grow and raise and nurture. To feed. To caretake. That's part of what was so hard. Knowing I couldn't have kids. I'd just always been programmed to believe that was a natural part of me."

Cameron hesitated. He'd never been afraid of wading into touchy waters, but this time, he desperately wanted to say the right thing. It's not like he knew anything about infertility. Or that he had any way to make her loss any less painful. But he had to find something right to say. The jerk she'd married had made her feel less than a woman, as if she were less than whole because of those "skinny tubes."

"*Chère,* I think you were a born nurturer. Just like your mother said. But I don't think that's just about children. It's about everything and everyone around you. Always will be. Although…"

"Although what?"

"Although I think there's a definite danger you could get overrun by cats." There, he'd made her smile. "If you started adopting elephants…well, the potential problems boggle the mind."

And there. He'd made her really laugh now. Feeling high on those successes, he pressed toward touchier ground. "I'm relieved you went for the divorce," he murmured, and kissed her forehead. "I'm sorry that he was such a blind idiot and hurt you. But if he hadn't had all those stupid ideas, who knows, maybe you'd have stuck with him. And then I'd never have found you."

"You think it's fate we found each other when we did?"

Her voice was getting sleepier, her cheek rooting for just the right place on his shoulder. "Not fate," he said quietly, bluntly. "Love. The kind of love that's actually freeing for us both. I mean—I already have two kids, so I don't need to start a formal family all over again. This is perfect. I'm a free spirit. So are you. We can both do anything, go anywhere we want. There's nothing to hold us down. Nothing to hold us back."

She seemed to go very still when he said the

"love" word, but she didn't immediately answer. Moments later, he realized she'd fallen asleep.

That was okay, he told himself. He just wanted to reassure her that he loved her for *her*. Maybe he'd hoped she would say something to indicate she wanted him to stick around in her life. But she'd just revealed that huge hole in her heart. Rome wasn't built in a day. Maybe she needed to think about that "love" word for a while. They had time yet.

Surely they still had time yet.

"Girls. Could you keep quiet for a full three seconds?" Both girls whirled around in surprise at her sharp tone. She never yelled at them. She never yelled at anyone, but darn it, August had blown in on a hot, mean wind. A few days ago she'd picked up a stomach bug she couldn't seem to shake. The cats were crabby; she hadn't been sleeping; and the girls had been talking for hours about school coming, boys, clothes, boys and then more boys.

"We need to make some more insect repellent. Remember the recipe? Ten parts lavender, ten parts geranium, five parts clove—"

"Hey, I remember it, Vi, not to worry."

"All right then, if you two'll make up two dozen of those vial—" She tried to finish the sentence, couldn't. Suddenly every smell in the Herb Haven seemed to fill her nostrils. She loved those smells. Every single one of them. Always had, always would. But just then, she put a hand over her mouth and ran like a bat out of hell for the back bathroom.

Twenty minutes later she decided that she wouldn't die, even found the strength to fumble in the medicine cabinet for her spare toothbrush and toothpaste. She worked up a good foam as she stared in the mirror. Her cheeks were pinch-pink, her eyes bright, her hair wild as a witch's but certainly glossy and healthy. Yet over the past week, she'd found an excuse to cry every day and hurl at least once.

Of course, crying was nothing new. She cried for the national anthem and for dog food commercials. But usually her stomach was cast iron. Last night they'd had fish with a spinach sauce and peachy sweet potatoes. Nothing a normal man would eat, but Cameron, par for Cameron, ate anything she put in front of him and asked for seconds. For herself, they were old favorites, comfort foods, no matter how weird they might be for someone else. Nothing, for damn sure, to inspire an upset tummy.

If she didn't have those skinny tubes, she might fear she was pregnant.

"Hey, Violet." Barbara rapped on the bathroom door. "We think you should go up to the house. Just forget all this. We'll make up the vials and those sachet things and handle the customers."

"You just want to talk about boys."

"Yeah, so? Go on. Go lie down or something."

She didn't want to go home. Cameron was up

there packing. He wasn't leaving for another couple of days, but the lavender harvest was over and it was not as if he could get all his stuff ready in a second. Between her missed period and her upset tummy and the insanely radiant cheeks she kept seeing in the mirror, Violet kept finding the "pregnancy" word sneaking into her mind. But skinny tubes didn't suddenly disappear, so she figured she was simply emotionally upset about his leaving.

"I'm not leaving you two kids alone in the shop," she said firmly.

Barbara opened the door, took one look and popped a bubble. "Yeah, you are." She aimed her thumb at the house in a clear-cut order. "Go on. It's hot. Go drink some lemonade or something."

Violet winced. "Don't say lemonade. Don't even think it out loud."

That's it. They pushed her out. And the heat was too searing and sticky to just stand there, so she had to traipse up to the house. The back door was open, the phone ringing, but hell's bells, the phone was always ringing. She opened the refrigerator and then just leaned into the cold smoky air with a sigh.

"Oh, God. Let me waste some electricity along with you." Cameron suddenly appeared from the dining room, shirtless and shoeless, just wearing low-slung khaki shorts and carrying packing tape. Now, though, he tossed the tape and hiked over to the open refrigerator. Faster than lightning, he dropped a soft, lingering kiss on her mouth. "Mmm. Fresh tooth-paste. What an aphrodisiac."

"I hate to say this, Lachlan, but you could find an aphrodisiac in a dust bunny." Oh, God. Even that light kiss and she was not only fine again, but her pulse was soaring like a hummingbird's. He'd changed her so much. Healed her. Made her feel like a whole woman again. And all because of those long, wicked nights and wild, sneaky kisses. Because of the way he loved her.

And the way she loved him back.

"Have you been out to our lavender? You know how it needs to be cut back, hard, as soon as the crop's taken. Well, old Filbert and the crew finished an hour ago. She's all tied up and pretty again."

Bad news. She closed the refrigerator door—after filling a cup full of ice—and headed for the couch in the living room. It was too hot to stand up. Too hot to hear bad news anywhere near that bright, happy sunlight. "You talked to Jeunnesse?"

"Yup." He didn't sit on the couch, instead, pulled up the old round ottoman and plunked down, facing her. "You know what has to happen now. I've tested all I can here. The rest has to happen in a bigger lab."

"I know."

"The next part of the testing takes time. Perfumes have a top note, a middle note and a base note. Lavender is used for all three. But the top note is usually the most volatile—the scent you pick up when you first put on perfume. And the base note—that's the scent that lingers even hours after you've been wearing the perfume.''

He was talking as if she didn't know these things. As if he believed he needed to carefully cover them again. He was looking at her as if she were some kind of fragile treasure. Searching her face the way he'd searched her face for days—even though she'd never told him, and never would, how strangely sick she'd been.

''The middle note in the perfume isn't so much about smell. It's about staying power. About chemistry. It's what makes one perfume last and another completely dissipate. It's what makes the best perfumes endure. And the right lavender is the key to that enduring power. It's what we're hoping your lavender has.''

She had no idea why he was telling her this. She knew it all. He knew it all. Somehow, though, every darn time Cam brought all this up again, all she could think of was how something was terribly wrong with her. Because unlike a good lavender, she seemed to have no enduring power for men. It wasn't just Simpson who'd left her.

Cam was leaving her now, too.

Simpson, she'd just loved. But Cameron was about to take her heart and soul with him. It was definitely some kind of flaw in her—she just seemed to attract men who didn't want to stay. For three years now, she'd blamed her infertility, but Cam had certainly proven that theory wrong, because he didn't care if she could have kids or not. He'd made it more than clear that he needed no more children.

"Vi, I *have* to go back to France. To the Jeunnesse labs."

"Of course you do." Because her voice sounded so hollow, she said more strongly, "I've known that from the start."

"There's a good staff of chemists there, and they can run most of the tests. But I know the lavender. I need to take charge of it."

"Cam, why are you telling me this? I've known from the beginning that you were only going to be here for a few weeks. We both knew."

"I just want to be sure you realize…that this isn't about wanting to leave you. It's just about the work." He waited, as if hoping she'd ask him something, say something.

And Violet knew exactly what he wanted to hear, so she put on her best ultraviolet smile and touched his cheek with love. "Didn't I tell you I never wanted ties?" she asked fiercely. "I love you, Cameron Lachlan. Just the way you are. Just the way we've been together. I wouldn't have given up a second of our summer for the world."

She saw his jaw clamp tight, and a light seemed to deaden in his eyes, but she couldn't fathom what else he might conceivably have wanted her to say. "There's no reason we can't see each other again," he said.

"I hope we do. But I don't want you worried about it." She couldn't tie him down. Wouldn't. Cam was who he was, a heart-free vagabond, a lover and a giver and a healer of women—but he'd tried marriage before, already had two daughters. He'd been terribly unhappy, and if there was one thing she wanted for this man who'd become her whole world, it was to love him. There was no way she'd ask him for anything he hadn't clearly offered.

"Have you picked a time to leave?" she asked lightly.

He nodded, then had to swallow as if something thick were stuck in his throat. "Tomorrow morning at daybreak. I can't wait longer than that."

So, Violet thought. Now I know the exact minute my heart's going to be broken for all time.

Eleven

Cameron watched his daughter's Jeep bounce out of his driveway. It had rained the last five days in September. His gravel driveway could have been renamed Mud Puddle Avenue. He waved another goodbye to Miranda and Kate.

The two girls were ecstatic he'd quit Jeunnesse and come home from France for good. They'd both asked about living with him—which could happen, if their mother agreed. He wasn't that sure what the girls really wanted or needed yet, but in the meantime he was less than two hours from their home. They could visit him anytime they wanted, especially now that Miranda had a driver's license.

When the car rounded the curve out of sight, he stuck his hands in his jeans pockets and aimed for the old shake-shingled cottage. The surrounding woods were starting to change color, picking up tips of gold and vermilion and bronze. The brook, at the back of the property, glistened in the sunlight. He took in a long clean breath, wanting to feel like he belonged here.

He didn't.

He wanted to. He'd loved the place when he bought it, even though at the time it was only to have a house close to his daughters for their visits here. And he'd quit Jeunnesse once he'd finished Violet's business and knew she was going to be set up any way she wanted to be in the future. At that point, though, he knew he no longer wanted to continue with that job. The work had been good to him and for him, but was nothing remotely what he wanted in his life anymore.

He'd thought—perhaps crazily—that he could recapture the feeling he had with Violet. He wanted that feeling of belonging. Of roots. He wanted a red barn and a stone fence. Rocks. Insane neighbors. A place private enough to make wild love in the moonlight with his one and only lover.

He stomped up the porch steps and pushed open the door, thinking darkly that he wanted a woman who cried at the drop of a hat, who made strange and wonderful food, who took in no end of cats and neighbors, who wore Victorian lace and neon-orange underpants.

Nothing but lonely silence greeted him in the house.

It was funny, but coming home, he'd made all kinds of foolish assumptions. For sure, he hadn't blindly assumed that Violet was ready to talk about wild, crazy things like *marriage*. But it was going to be so much easier to see her now, easier to talk, easier to be together. He'd planned to try a relentless romantic assault by courting her in all the old-fashioned ways.

It had never once occurred to him that she wouldn't answer his notes or phone calls.

In the brick kitchen he poured the last mug of coffee from this morning's pot. The brew was now thicker than mud, not that he cared.

One of the girls had left a pink sock, and a couple of teen girl magazines zooed up the pristine neatness of the place, but otherwise there was nothing inside but wood and a stone fireplace and big leather furniture and silence.

It was tough, accepting that he'd misunderstood everything that mattered. He'd *thought* he was ready to settle down. He'd *thought* he was ready to finally belong. He'd *thought* he'd finally come to terms with his father's legacy of fearing a place could own him instead of the other way around. Instead, he'd discovered that his lack of interest in a home had nothing to do with his father.

All this time, it had simply been about finding a woman he wanted to belong with.

He got it now. He got it all. Except, he couldn't seem to believe that he'd come this far, hurt this much, finally found himself—and found her—and then had to accept that he'd lost her.

The phone rang, a shock of sound that made him whip around and spill a few coffee drops from his mug. He grabbed the receiver and tucked it under his ear.

"Cameron Lachlan?"

He heard the woman's scream, and immediately recognized the voice as Daisy Campbell, Violet's oldest sister. He'd always liked her. She was breathtaking, an exotic beauty, fiercely independent, her own woman. She'd been living with some artist in the south of France, which was how she'd been in his "Jeunnesse neighborhood" these last years. But the thing was, they'd always gotten along well, so it was nearly impossible to connect the cool-eyed beauty with the woman yelling at him across the ocean.

"Lachlan, did I or did I not tell you that I'd kill you if you broke my sister's heart?!"

"What?"

"I *told* you she was vulnerable. I *told* you to be

good to her or to leave her alone. I thought you were a decent guy!''

''Um, I could have sworn I was, too—''

''Well, I'm leaving Provence for good and coming back across the Atlantic. And the very minute I get home, I'm going to kill you. I'm not sure how yet. I've never killed anything before. But where I grew up, buster, a man didn't get a woman pregnant and then take off.''

''*What?*'' This time he'd been lifting the mug to his mouth. Only, he dropped it. Sludgy hot coffee spattered all over the place. The ceramic mug broke in a half dozen pieces. ''What did you say?'

''Give me a break, Lachlan! I don't care whether she told you or not. If you weren't going to use some protection, you knew perfectly well you were taking a risk. You know damn well how babies are made!''

''But not for your sister.'' He couldn't seem to catch his breath, couldn't seem to think.

''What's that supposed to mean, not for my sister?''

He opened his mouth to answer but then couldn't. In a flash he realized that Violet had never told her family about the infertility, how her ex-husband had treated her, none of it. She loved her sisters, talked about them all the time. So it must have hurt more than she could bear to even try to share it.

Except with him.

She'd cared enough to share it with *him*. The

thought registered, but it was pretty hard to concentrate. Daisy was still winding up, and beauty or no beauty, she could yell like a drill sergeant. "Don't even try playing any stupid games with me, Lachlan. I've heard every excuse a man can make up for irresponsibility. I can smell them. I *told* you my sister was vulnerable. All I asked was that you be decent to her, be nice, be fair. If you two ended up in the sack...all right, I admit I thought you'd like each other. I even admit I thought an affair was a good idea for our Vi. But to get her pregnant, you scoundrel, you creep, you turkey, you unfeeling, revolting, irresponsible... Cameron, why the hell aren't you answering me?"

"Daisy, do me a favor and don't tell your sister that you called me."

For the first time since the phone call started, Daisy stopped frothing fire and brimstone. Confusion silenced her—although not for long. "Do you a favor? Do *you* a favor? Did you want me to do you that favor before or after I murder you?!"

He didn't mean to hang up on her. He just forgot she was there. Violet? Pregnant with his child? And once those wheels started spinning, they seemed to pick up speed nonstop.

He was in upstate New York, not Vermont. He had fresh food in the fridge, a coffeepot on, a load of clothes heaped in the washer, bills waiting to be paid on the counter, a dentist appointment two days from now. He couldn't just take off.

Fifteen minutes later he started the car.

If everything went perfectly—no pit or food stops, no construction zones—he could make the trip in four hours.

Naturally he ran into three construction zones and one minor accident. He combined a pit stop with a run on fast food and strong coffee. Even this early in fall, the sun dropped fast. By the time he crossed the border into Vermont, dusk had fallen. Blustery clouds stole the last of daylight, and then there was only that quiet blacktop and him.

He remembered the rolling hills. The stone fences. The white steepled churches in White Hills. The pretty red barns and winding roads. Every familiar sight heightened both his anticipation and his fear.

He pulled into her yard after nine, not realizing until then how long his heart had been pounding, or that the burger he'd wolfed down was still sitting in his stomach like a clunky ball. Yellow lights glowed in her windows. A cornstalk scarecrow sat at the bottom of her porch steps, keeping two of the cats company. A pair of giant pumpkins, still uncarved, framed her door. Pruning shears sat on the porch swing, not put away.

He vaulted the steps of the porch, hiked toward the door and then abruptly stopped. Faster than lightning, he tucked, buttoned, straightened. Then he realized that, hell, he hadn't brushed his hair since he could even remember. And he should have shaved. Still…he'd come this far, and God knew Violet had seen him in worse shape than in an old black sweater and cords. So he knocked.

Nothing. No answer.

He knocked again, louder this time.

Still, there was no response. So he poked his head in. Smells immediately swarmed his senses—apples and cinnamons and cloves. A bowl of mums nested on the hearth. A copper pot held long, tall grasses and reeds. Lavender—naturally—hung upside down from the kitchen beams. Two cats spotted him, remembered him for the sucker he was and leaped down from the rockers to get petted.

Still, there was no sight of Violet, only the sound of her. She was singing from somewhere upstairs, assuming one could call the sounds emanating from her throat "singing." Her sister Daisy could scream like a shrew, where Vi's singing voice, he thought tenderly, resembled steel scratching steel—at a high pitch.

"Violet?" He had to let her know he was there, didn't want to scare her. "Vi?"

The caterwauling stopped. A hesitant voice called down, "Cameron?" But then followed through with a swift, "Don't answer that. Obviously you can't be Cameron."

Oh, God. It was like coming home. Only his ditsy

Violet could make irrational comments like that, and maybe he was crazy, maybe he was risking his heart and his life, but he took the stairs three at a time and galloped down the hall. He wouldn't have known positively where that ghastly operatic voice had been coming from, if there hadn't been puffs of fragrant steam dancing out the open door of the master bath.

He leaned both arms against the doorjamb, trying to catch his breath. Yet almost immediately he realized that he would likely never catch his breath because his heart had completely stopped.

She was in the bathtub. No longer singing the blues, just sunken in the warm water to the tips of her nipples, her long hair twisted and clipped out of the way. Two cats sat on the porcelain rim, balanced precariously but acting the part of sentinels. The bathwater wasn't sudsy. In fact, he could see clearly to her pale white skin under the surface, the long slim legs, the white curve of her hip, the plump breasts. And the tummy.

His gaze fell on her tummy and his heart stopped all over again.

"Hi," she said, as if she regularly greeted strange men in her bathtub. Now, though, he knew her well. Doing the unpredictable, the ditsy, the flaky, was how she'd learned to protect herself—especially from men wanting to look too closely. He wasn't fooled anymore. He could hear the uncertainty in her

voice and see the gamut of emotions in her eyes.
Pain. Longing. Love.

How could he have missed that the love was there?

"Smells great in here," he murmured.

"It should. It's my personal recipe for a bath to
take away your cares, no matter how heavy your
heart is. It's got a little lavender, a little marjoram, a
little peppermint and some secret ingredients I'll
never tell anyone." She looked at him with those
clear, soft, vulnerable eyes and then took a breath.

"Except you, Cam. I'll tell you. I mix a little lily
of the valley and jasmine in there. That's my secret."

"Aha," he said. And heeled off his right shoe.
Then his left. His black sweater peeled off by a miracle. It had to be a miracle, because he was too fum-
ble-fingered to do it himself. "I like the tummy."

She glanced down. "I've really been on a milk-
shake binge."

"I don't think that's the reason for the tummy."

"No?" She sucked in a breath when he peeled off
his cords and shorts. "Um, Cameron. You're going
to smell like flowers if you come in here."

"I'd care about that if I were a sissy. But I happen
to be a tough guy. A tough guy always does what a
tough guy has to do." The cats scattered when he
stepped in. The water whooshed up to the top of the
tub and splashed over. She didn't notice or look. She
only looked at him, pulled her knees up.

"You couldn't get a bath closer to home?"

"Well, that's the problem, chère. It took me this long, not to take a bath, but to realize that this *is* home."

Total silence fell for a moment. He sank in, knee to knee, eye to eye, and reached out a hand. She folded her fingers with his. "I didn't think you wanted a home, Cameron Lachlan."

"I don't know if I ever told you about my dad. I loved him. He wasn't a bad guy, nothing like that. But he built his whole life around possessions. Things owned him instead of the other way around. He was never home for us. He never had time for us."

"I'm sorry."

"I don't want you to be sorry. I just needed you to understand how I turned into a vagabond. I just never wanted that to happen to me. I wanted people to matter, not things. I wanted the freedom to love people, not things." He laved her feet, since they were easy to reach. And her knees. He got her knees really, really clean. "And then I met you. And lost you. And realized I was doing exactly what he did wrong. Putting a barrier between myself and who I wanted to spend time with, who I wanted to love. Who I needed in my life."

He moved up from the knees, to those long, silky white thighs. Her phone rang. It seemed a measure of how well he knew her, and them, that neither even blinked or made any effort to answer it. Phones were always going to ring in this house. They'd wait.

"I quit Jeunnesse. Came back to my place in New York, saw my girls. But the whole time I kept thinking about making a whole different kind of life. I've got the money to buy the land, put in a big five-hundred acres of lavender. It'd be adventurous, challenging. Hard work, but still a lot of free traveling time in the winter. Time to be impulsive any way a couple might want to be. Of course, we have to find a house-sitter for the cats. And obviously it's not your usual life—it'd only work for people who really liked the land, got a charge out of getting their hands dirty—"

"So...you came back for the land, did you?"

"Nope." He could see that haunted look leaving her eyes. And she wasn't backing away from him. But she didn't move toward him.

"You always sounded so positive, Cam. That you didn't want to settle down."

"I don't want to settle down. I want to live with you and be your lover. Forever. I don't want to *settle* for anything. I want to create exactly the life that works-for us. I was going to say for the two of us—but maybe for the three or four or five of us, if for any reason the family somehow grew."

Again she went still, seemed to even stop breathing. "Daisy called you, didn't she?"

He didn't directly answer that, because this wasn't

about her sister or anything her sister had said to him. It was about the two of them. And to make sure he had her attention, he took her warm, slippery hands in his. "I don't think it's a good idea for a woman to marry a guy who has nearly grown children...at least until you've met the children. I'm totally positive you'd get on with them like a house afire, but they *are* teenagers, which means they stay up nights trying to think up new ways to make adults' lives difficult. For myself, though, I've always liked kids. Nice kids, wild kids, difficult kids, doesn't matter to me. I'd love more."

"Lachlan, that isn't at all what you said before."

"I know, I know. I wasn't exactly lying before. But I was trying to make sure you know I loved you for *you*. That you were what mattered to me, not whether you could have kids or not. I love you first. I want you first."

Tears started to well up in her soft eyes, so he started talking faster.

"Violet, you're probably ten times more woman than I can handle, but I'd like to try. But I want you to absolutely know that my loving you has nothing to do with kids. If you want some, we can adopt or foster, or try working with those skinny tubes...hell, maybe we can just take in more cats. I don't know. I don't care. I just care that we work together to find choices that are right for us."

She took a long, shaky breath. "It's possible that this tummy isn't caused by too many milkshakes."

"I thought the skinny tubes were pretty much a for-sure problem."

"So did I. Every doctor I went to told me my chances of conception were minuscule." Her fingertips caressed his. Her gaze seemed to caress his face at the same time. "You must have awfully determined little seeds in there, Lachlan."

"I prefer to think of them as skillful. And smart enough to go after what they want." He wanted to draw her into his arms, right there, right then. They had a lifetime to finish all this talking business, and the old-fashioned tub was big, but not necessarily big enough for the rest of the night he had planned. Yet he had to say gently, "You should have told me you were pregnant, chère."

"I wanted to and I would have. But I had to think about how, Cam. I never wanted you to feel trapped. Nothing works when a person feels trapped. And I love you. Of everyone in the universe, Cameron Lachlan, I so want you to be happy. I want you to have what you need in your life."

There, now. He drew her on top of him. Warm water sloshed on the floor, but still he finally had her, breast to breast, tummy to tummy. Heart to heart. "That's easy, then, because what I need is you. In my life, all my life."

"That's a two-way street. I love you so much. And

I want you in my life, all my life,'' she whispered, and blessed him with an eyes-closed, drowning-defying, promise-invoking kiss. When they came up for air, his eyes were moist and hers were dry.

It was going to be a hell of a thing, if she turned him into an emotional kind of guy. Chemists were supposed to be rational, calm, cold types, but somehow Cameron didn't think that was going to work. Not anymore.

He'd always tried to be careful, not to let anything own him. Yet Violet owned his heart—and it was the best thing that had ever happened to him. Of course, that was just today.

They had a lifetime to explore all they could be together.

*   *   *   *   *

Watch for Daisy's story, coming soon from Silhouette Desire.

DYNASTIES: THE DANFORTHS

A family of prominence...
tested by scandal, sustained by passion.

COWBOY CRESCENDO
(Silhouette Desire #1591)

by Cathleen Galitz

Newly hired nanny Heather Burroughs quickly
won over Toby Danforth's young son with her
warmth and humor, but Toby's affection was
harder to tap into. This sizzling cowboy was
still reeling from his disastrous divorce and
certainly wasn't looking for a new bride.
Could Heather lasso this lone rancher
and get him to settle down?

Available July 2004
at your favorite retail outlet.

Enjoy
Barbara McCauley's

SECRETS!

*Hidden passions are revealed
in this next exciting installment
of the bestselling series.*

MISS PRUITT'S
PRIVATE LIFE
(Silhouette Desire #1593)

Brother to the groom, Evan Carter was
immediately attracted to a friend of the bride:
sexy TV sensation Marcy Pruitt. While helping
to pull the wedding together, they found
themselves falling into a scandalous affair.
But when Miss Pruitt's private life became
public knowledge, would their shared passion
result in a wedding of their own?

*Available July 2004
at your favorite retail outlet.*

BABY AT *HIS* CONVENIENCE

by
Kathie DeNosky

(Silhouette Desire #1595)

Katie Andrews wants a strong, sexy
man to father her child. When former
marine sergeant major Jeremiah Gunn
walks into her café, Katie believes she's
found the perfect candidate. Trouble is,
Jeremiah has some conditions of his
own before he'll agree to give Katie
what she wants—including turning sweet,
shy Katie into the type of brazenly
uninhibited woman he's used to.

Available July 2004
at your favorite retail outlet.

Silhouette® *Desire*®

COMING NEXT MONTH

#1591 COWBOY CRESCENDO—Cathleen Galitz
Dynasties: The Danforths
Newly hired nanny Heather Burroughs quickly won over Toby Danforth's young son with her warmth and humor, but Toby's affection was harder to tap into. This sexy cowboy was still reeling from his disastrous divorce and wasn't looking to involve himself in any type of relationship. Could Heather lasso this lone rancher into settling down?

#1592 BEST-KEPT LIES—Lisa Jackson
The McCaffertys
Green-eyed P.I. Kurt Striker was hired to protect Randi McCafferty and her baby against a mysterious attacker. After being run off the road by this veiled villain, Randi had the strength to survive any curve life threw her. But did she have the power to steer clear of her irresistibly rugged protector?

#1593 MISS PRUITT'S PRIVATE LIFE—Barbara McCauley
Secrets!
Brother to the groom Evan Carter was immediately attracted to friend of the bride and well-known television personality Marcy Pruitt. While helping to pull the wedding together, they found themselves falling into a scandalous affair. But when Miss Pruitt's private life became public knowledge, would their shared passion result in a wedding of their own?

#1594 STANDING OUTSIDE THE FIRE—Sara Orwig
Stallion Pass: Texas Knights
Former Special Forces colonel and sexy charmer Boone Devlin clashed with Erin Frye over the ranch she managed and he had recently inherited. The head-to-head confrontation soon turned into head-over-heels passion. This playboy made it clear that nothing could tame him—but could an unexpected pregnancy change that?

#1595 BABY AT *HIS* CONVENIENCE—Kathie DeNosky
She wanted a strong, sexy man to father her child—and waitress Katie Andrews had decided that Jeremiah Gunn fit the bill exactly. Trouble was, Jeremiah had some terms of his own before he'd agree to give Katie what she wanted…and that meant becoming his mistress.…

#1596 BEYOND CONTROL—Bronwyn Jameson
Free-spirited Kree O'Sullivan had never met a sexier man than financier Sebastian Sinclair. Even his all-business, take-charge attitude intrigued her. Just once she wanted Seb to go wild—for her. But when the sizzling attraction between them began to loosen *her* restraints, she knew passion would soon spiral out of control…for both of them.

SDCNM0604